MURDER AT THE MANSIONS

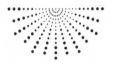

MURDER AT THE MANSIONS

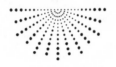

SARA ROSETT

MURDER AT THE MANSIONS

A 1920s Historical Mystery

Book Seven in the High Society Lady Detective series

Published by McGuffin Ink

ISBN: 978-1-950054-40-4

Copyright © 2022 by Sara Rosett

Cover Design: ebooklaunch.com

Floorplan and Illustration: Joanna Pasek with Qamber Designs

Editing: Historical Editorial

❀ Created with Vellum

SOUTH REGENT MANSIONS

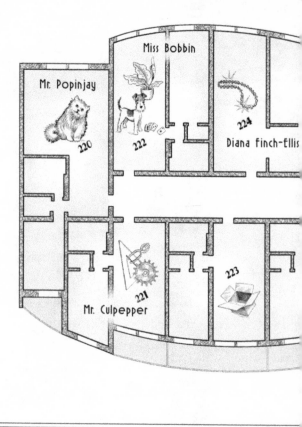

Mr. Popinjay

Miss Bobbin

220

222

224

Diana finch-Ellis

Mr. Culpepper

221

223

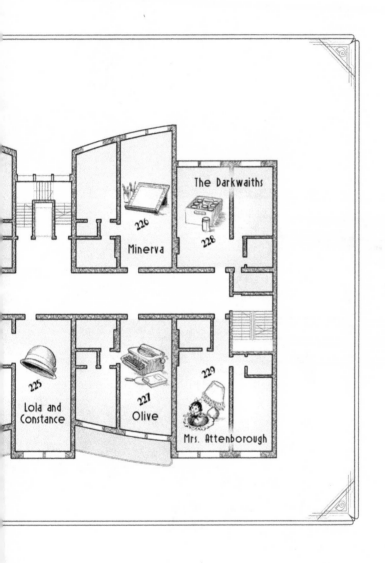

The Darkwaiths

226

Minerva

228

225

Lola and
Constance

227

Olive

229

Mrs. Attenborough

*ebruary 1924*

I hurried through the foggy gloom toward the faint golden rectangle that was the entrance to the South Regent Mansions. A burst of chilly drizzle hit the nape of my neck and made me momentarily regret my fashionable bob. I pushed through the glass doors and entered the warmth of the lobby, which felt as if I'd moved from the dark wings of a theater into a spotlight at center stage. A crystal chandelier glittered overhead, its sparkling facets reflected in the Carrara marble flooring and in the mirrors that lined the white wainscoted walls. Workmen had been in earlier in the day to paint the back stairs, and the potent smell of fresh paint permeated the air.

I was a few steps behind a delivery boy who announced to the porter in piping tones, "Delivery for the Darkwaiths."

I slowed my steps at the mention of the name. Everyone was curious about the Darkwaiths, who supposedly resided in flat 228.

The head porter for South Regent Mansions, Evans, loomed behind the counter, his walrus-like physique filling the alcove as he spoke to Mrs. Attenborough. She glanced over her shoulder and down her long nose at the delivery boy, giving him a look that was as cold as the icy rain outside. "In my day, children knew better than to interrupt."

The delivery boy, whose flat cap was so large that it covered the tips of his ears, halted, his thin arms braced around a box that was wider than his chest.

Mrs. Attenborough turned back to the porter. "As I was saying, my rubbish bin wasn't returned until noon. According to the schedule, the bins are to be placed in the rubbish lift by eight o'clock, and they will be emptied and returned no later than eleven each morning."

Evans smoothed his mustache, which curved down on each side of his mouth and only emphasized his likeness to a walrus, then nodded the boy in the direction of the lift as he reached for a pen. "I'll note it down, Mrs. Attenborough."

The delivery boy spun away from the porter's alcove, his short legs scissoring along the stretch of scarlet carpet that ran from the building's front door to the lift, which was waiting on the ground floor.

I nodded to Evans and Mrs. Attenborough as I skirted around them and increased my pace, scooting along the plush carpet so I could ride up in the lift with the delivery boy. I didn't want to miss an opportunity to quiz him about the mysterious Darkwaiths.

He was lowering the box to the ground so he could close the lift's accordion-like gate. I stepped on and gripped the metal. "Allow me. Your hands are quite full." The crisscross metal slats shifted as I stretched the gate across the opening. I latched it and turned to the lift panel. "Second floor, I believe?"

He nodded, hefted the box higher in his arms, and receded into the back corner.

"That's my floor as well." The lift was slow and creaky, but I only had a few moments before we reached our destination.

At my words, the delivery boy's eyes widened as he focused on me for a moment, then he adjusted his grip on the box and dropped his gaze.

It wasn't surprising he didn't speak. A few encounters with the Mrs. Attenboroughs of the world had probably taught him he was better off remaining silent in the presence of adults. I tried again. "Do you bring deliveries often for the Darkwaiths?"

He nodded.

"How often?"

He lifted his chin so he could look up at me from under the brim of his cap. "Twice a month."

"That's interesting. Does someone take the deliveries from you?"

As my conversational tone continued, his shoulders relaxed an inch. "No, miss. I leave it outside the door."

"Really?" I infused the word with as much warmth as I could.

"I put the box on the mat outside the door and knock

before I leave."

The lift trudged to a stop with a little bounce, which was unusual. The repairman had been in today to work on the lift, which had been rather unreliable, often refusing to budge from the ground floor when the call button was pushed on one of the upper floors. "They don't want you to carry the box in? It looks quite heavy," I said over the metal clangs as I slid back the gate.

He shrugged one skinny shoulder. "No, miss. Them's the instructions."

The items in the box were staples—tins of tea, packets of crackers, and a jar of fish paste, plus a few other tins turned so the labels weren't visible. "It doesn't look like much food."

He looked at the box as if he'd never considered what was in it. "They must like it. It's always the same thing, every fortnight. Must be somebody old. Old folks don't eat much." He politely waited for me to exit the lift first. I said goodbye as I stepped out into the corridor, which had the same decor as the lobby, pristine white walls and a scarlet runner. The odor of paint was stronger here too. The door that led to the back stairs at the far end of the hall was propped open, and the workmen had left a sawhorse in front of it with an unnecessary note tacked to it that read, *Wet Paint*.

I paused at my door and called after the boy, "What shop do you deliver for?"

He turned back as he shifted the box against his chest. "Belmont's."

I took pity on him and stopped asking questions. The

box did look quite heavy. I took my time with my key so I could watch him out of the corner of my eye. He did indeed put the box down on the mat in front of 228, then he knocked and returned to the lift, doffing his cap at me as he went by.

I smiled back at him as I slipped into my flat but lingered at the door, leaving it open an inch so I could watch the door to 228. The gate clanked as the boy closed it, then there was a mechanical *whoosh* as it rattled downward. Silence settled along the corridor as thick as the layer of fog outside. I waited, feeling a bit silly, but I'd lived in the flat for several months and I'd never seen any of the Darkwaiths —and neither had anyone else, as far as Minerva and I could make out.

Minerva's flat was across the hall from me. She was the one who had piqued my curiosity about the Darkwaiths. I'd managed to meet everyone else on the second floor. I had to admit that it was rather odd to have never seen the occupants of a flat on the same floor as mine. Minerva and I had speculated about the possible residents of 228. My bet was that there was only one resident, a recluse. Minerva, who lived next door to the Darkwaiths in 226, reported that she had never heard any noise through the walls and favored the theory that an invalid lived there.

The peal of the telephone rang out from my sitting room, but I ignored it and stayed where I was, my gaze fixed on the door to 228. The box sat on the mat as my telephone continued to jangle. Perhaps it was Minerva, calling about dinner tonight to say she wanted me to come early. The sharp clangor of the telephone cut off in the midst of the seventh ring. I continued to watch 228.

After a few moments, the telephone bell went again. I let out a little huff of irritation. Clearly the caller didn't intend to give up. I lingered another moment or two, but the door to 228 remain closed. I shut my door and went down the short hallway, passing the tiny kitchen on the way to the sitting room.

I set my handbag down on the desk and answered.

"Hello, old bean. How are you?"

"Jasper!" I settled on the corner of my desk. "How marvelous to hear from you. Is anything wrong?"

"No. Why?"

"I thought we wouldn't speak until you returned to London."

"I decided to make use of this handy new-fangled invention, the telephone, so I could hear your voice. I find Edinburgh strangely flat. The Royal Mile would be much more enchanting with you by my side."

"So your book auction hasn't begun yet," I said, and Jasper's laugh came through the line over the static. "When it kicks off tomorrow, I'm sure you'll have plenty to keep you busy. And, although it would be lovely to be there with you, I'm in the middle of a case."

"How is your inquiry going?"

"Quite well. Everything seems completely aboveboard. Rather boring, actually."

"Don't worry. I'm sure you'll find something intriguing before long. You usually do, old bean."

"I don't see how looking into some of the most respected

charities in London could possibly be surprising, but at this point I'd welcome it. Financial records are rather tedious, you know. Thank goodness I did Father's accounts at the vicarage for years. Otherwise, I'd be hopelessly lost." I slipped off the desk and moved around to my chair. "What do you have your eye on for the auction tomorrow?"

"There's a lovely copy of a Mercedes Quero. First edition."

"Do get it if you can."

"I intend to. I'm quite fond of lady detectives, both fictional and corporeal."

"Delighted to hear that."

Silence flowed over the line for a few seconds. Things had shifted for Jasper and me at Christmas. He'd been rather secretive in the past, but that was over. I had no doubt that his only reason for traveling to Edinburgh was to go on a book-buying expedition. However, now that the barrier of his reticence had come down, everything had changed between us. I felt as if before Christmas, we'd been moving around in a shrubbery maze, catching only glimpses of each other. Now it was as if we were standing on a wide plane with the horizon stretching out all around us. We were feeling our way through this new phase, and I don't think either of us was sure of the course we should take.

I swiveled in my desk chair as I cast around for something else to say, but my elbow bumped my new Remington portable typewriter and knocked off a notepad I'd propped on top with a reminder scribbled on the first page. "Oh botheration!" I picked up the notepad from the floor. "I must go out again. Minerva's asked me to dinner this evening, and I promised to bring a bottle of wine. I'd better go now. I'm supposed to be at Minerva's in half an hour, and I must unearth my umbrella."

"I'll ring off then, so you can brave the elements." His voice lost some of its usual jaunty tone and softened. "See you the day after tomorrow, old thing."

"I look forward to it."

"As do I."

I put the receiver down slowly. Despite the dreary day, inside I felt sunny and warm. I didn't even mind the thought of going out again. I extracted my umbrella and a scarf from the closet in my bedroom, picked up my handbag, then stepped out into the hallway. The mat in front of 228 was empty. The box was gone, and I'd missed it, which was thoroughly annoying. I'd had a chance to get a definite answer about who lived there, and I'd failed.

I punched the button to recall the lift. At least now I knew that someone in 228 received a delivery every two weeks. Surely I could catch a glimpse of one of the inhabitants now that I knew the schedule. All I had to do was watch for the delivery boy and make sure my telephone was not in its cradle next time.

Mrs. Attenborough still stood in the porter's alcove, tapping the porter's logbook with a finger as she emphasized her point. I gave them a quick nod as I passed but didn't slow.

I didn't think it was possible that the fog could have become denser, but it did seem to have thickened in the short amount of time I'd been indoors.

The February weather had settled on the most miserable

combination—a heavy fog mixed with sudden spurts of frigid drizzle. The mist had descended on London at noon, cloaking the city and blurring the outlines of buildings, motor cars, and passersby, who splashed along the pavement, huddled under black umbrellas. The taut panels of the umbrellas emerged from the whitish murkiness dripping moisture and bobbed toward me like sea creatures breaking the surface of the ocean. Thankfully, I only had to walk one block to make my purchase, and I was back at South Regent Mansions in less than a quarter hour.

Evans had disengaged himself from Mrs. Attenborough by the time I'd returned. Through the haze of the mist, I could make out his rotund shape as he opened the door of a taxi that had pulled up to the twin yellow rectangles of the glass doors leading to the lobby. He held a large umbrella high to shelter one of the residents while the doorman opened the door of another motor that stood in front of the cab.

I recognized one of my second-floor neighbors, Dolores Mallory—or Lola, as she'd insisted I call her—as she stamped through the puddles to the taxi. She wore her mint-green coat and matching cloche. A white feather curled from the brim and swayed near her cheekbone.

I did a quick survey of the area to make sure no other residents were in sight, then quickened my pace. "Hello, Lola," I called.

She paused, poised to climb into the taxi.

Tiny freezing drops of icy water beat against my umbrella as I closed the distance. "Would you like to meet for tea tomorrow?"

She glanced over her shoulder, her alligator handbag swinging on her arm as she swiveled. "Yes, of course."

"Perhaps you'd like to come around to my flat?" Lola was my client, and she'd been quite clear that if I had news to share, I should make sure she was alone before I said anything.

"No, do come by our flat. Sorry, but I'm in quite a rush."

"Then I'll see you tomorrow."

The porter closed the door of the motor, and it splashed away. I dashed up the steps and into South Regent Mansions, shaking the droplets from my umbrella. I pulled the gate of the lift into place, all the while mentally filling in my calendar for tomorrow as the lift chugged upward. I had one more inquiry to make for Lola. I'd be able to complete it in the morning and return to the flat, where I could type out my brief report for her. I was in the process of learning to touch-type. It was slow going, but several hours should be sufficient.

The lift rattled to a stop with another springy bounce, and I checked my watch. I had just enough time to change my dress and freshen up before dinner.

A few minutes later, I crossed the hall to Minerva's flat. A spicy aroma wafted out when she opened the door. "Hello, Olive." She must have just returned from the newspaper office because she wore her rather severe jacket and skirt in a shade of gray that reminded me of the fog. Minerva had deep-set, hooded eyes with fashionably thin eyebrows and a long nose. Tonight her red cupid-bow lips parted in a quick, automatic smile, which was unlike her usual genuine greeting. "Come in. I'm glad you could make it. Our dinner party has dwindled to just us."

I handed her the wine. "That's disappointing."

"I'm glad, actually. Something happened today—something extremely disturbing that I must talk over with you."

CHAPTER TWO

s Minerva stepped back so I could enter the flat, her glance strayed over my shoulder, and an anxious look flickered across her features.

I looked back, but the hallway was empty, the red runner stretching away between the row of closed doors. "Something disturbing happened?"

She gave a sharp shake of her head and closed the door. "I'll tell you later. First, dinner."

I followed her into the flat. Even though I'd met Minerva recently, I knew her well enough to know she didn't toss around adjectives and adverbs like some of my flapper friends. To them, small annoying things like running out of pink champagne was *ghastly*. Parties that fell flat were *frightful* or *grim*. But Minerva didn't embellish her speech in that way. For her to use the word *disturbing* meant that something was very wrong. But I followed her cue and didn't press her. She'd tell me when she was ready.

Minerva stepped into the kitchen and opened a drawer. "Miss Bobbin has a sniffle and is staying in."

I motioned to the platter of curry on the counter. "Shall I carry this through?"

"Yes, please. Let me find the corkscrew. I'll be along in a moment."

"And Mr. Culpepper?" I went into the sitting room. Minerva's flat was on the opposite side of the building from mine. One of the best features of South Regent Mansions was its lovely oversized windows. Minerva's windows looked out on the back courtyard, a tiny concrete area where a few affluent residents paid extra to park their motors. The drapes were open, and ranks of imposing red brick buildings, all multistory service flats like South Regent Mansions, rose beyond the courtyard, their lit windows glowing in a fuzzy checkerboard pattern through the fog.

While Minerva's view wasn't quite as attractive as mine, which overlooked the park in front of the building, her flat was more spacious. I had the smallest floor plan with a kitchen, a sitting room, one bedroom, and a minuscule bath. Minerva's flat had a larger bedroom and dining room.

The dinner party cancelations must have been last-minute, because four places had been laid. I positioned the curry at the center of the table, under the modern chandelier with three circular tiers of narrow icicle-like crystals.

Minerva's voice floated out of the kitchen. "Mr. Culpepper had something come up at work and won't be able to join us."

"Then I'll have to hear about his latest invention next

time." Mr. Culpepper was a quiet sort. I'd been seated beside him at another of Minerva's dinner parties, and I'd found chatting with him arduous until I brought up the subject of gadgets and innovations. He told me about a recent invention, a rotor machine called Enigma model A, which sounded like a modified typewriter that produced code. It was something I knew would interest Jasper, so I'd asked Mr. Culpepper plenty of questions about it. Once on that subject, Mr. Culpepper had become quite a good conversationalist.

"Switch on the radio for us, will you?" Minerva asked. "I'm almost done here. Be out in a moment."

I went to the sitting room and switched on the radio. A blast of music from the Wireless Orchestra filled the room. I adjusted the volume so it was background music.

Minerva called out, "Take a look at the sketches on my desk and tell me what you think. I'm inking one, but the other is a draft. They're for next week's editions."

The sitting room had a sofa and two chairs grouped around the fireplace, but I knew Minerva spent most of her time on the other side of the room at the angled drafting desk, which she'd placed directly in front of the huge window.

Both of the drawings were of the familiar character of Beatrice, the Bright Young Person who regularly appeared in the cartoons that Minerva drew for *The Hullabaloo* newspaper. One sketch was done in pencil. With a few strokes, Minerva conveyed the elegant sweep of Beatrice's evening gown as she peered over her shoulder at her reflection in a full-length looking glass. It took me a second to decipher

Minerva's scrawled caption. *The back doesn't plunge nearly enough. I've already chopped off my hair. The only way I can shock people now is with the cut of my dress.*

I grinned and flipped it back to expose the second drawing. It was partially inked, with darker bold strokes covering some of the original pencil sketch. It depicted Beatrice in three side-by-side sketches. In the one on the left of the page, Beatrice was behind the wheel of a motor that was skimming down a country lane, her scarf waving out behind her. The sketch in the middle showed Beatrice on the golf course, her club at the apex of its swing. Faint pen strokes indicated the club had just swept through the air.

The third drawing, on the right, was of two plump matrons having tea. One of them said, "We're fortunate that our Beatrice isn't one of those lazy modern young people. She has several driving passions, you know."

I stepped back from the desk with a smile. "They're both excellent."

Minerva came into the room, carrying a wineglass in one hand and a platter in the other. "I've got to work on the caption for the one with the evening gown. I'm not quite satisfied with it. It's a bit long."

"Well, I like it," I said as she handed me the wineglass. "I look forward to seeing the final versions."

She placed the platter on the table. "Let me get my glass, and we can sit down."

As I turned away from the desk, I noticed a piece of paper that had fallen to the floor and picked it up. It was another sketch, but not of Beatrice. "Oh, a self-portrait," I said as Minerva came back in the room, turning it so she could see what I held. She'd emphasized her hooded eyes, exaggerated the arch of her eyebrows, lengthened her Grecian nose, and made her stylishly small rosebud mouth ridiculously miniature.

She laughed, a real smile lighting up her face. "Oh, that. I lost a bet with Cyril—one of the reporters. That's my forfeit. A caricature of myself, which my face is made for."

"Nonsense. Your features are intriguing. The paper should run it sometime."

"Heavens, no." She didn't exactly snatch it out of my hand, but she certainly didn't let me hang onto it. "I don't want people accosting me on the street to complain about the morals of flappers." She shoved it in a drawer in the sideboard.

"Does that happen often?"

"Definitely. I made the mistake of saying I drew the *Beatrice* cartoon at a dinner party once. I was lectured for most of the evening." She motioned me to a seat. "People make the mistake of believing that Beatrice and I are one and the same."

"That couldn't be further from the truth," I said as we sat down at the table.

Minerva handed me the platter of curry. "Quite. Beatrice is titled and affluent. I'm neither of those."

"I was thinking more along the lines of Beatrice being bored and mercurial. Anyone who knows you would never say either of those things about you."

"Thank you."

I passed the curry back to her. "Now tell me about this Cyril."

"Cyril? What about him?"

"Well, is he interesting? Any potential there?"

She frowned at me.

"A potential beau?" I clarified.

"Potential? With Cyril Buncombe?" She laughed, a full, deep laugh. "Only if I'm interested in a septuagenarian."

". . . but the phone continued to ring," I said, "and so I *had* to answer it. It was Jasper. When I returned, the box outside flat 228 was gone."

After a few beats of silence, Minerva, who had been pushing the last few bites of her curry back and forth across her plate, looked up. "Gone, you said?"

I could tell she'd had to reach back in her memory to grasp the thread of my story. Minerva had been distracted throughout dinner, and she hadn't shown even a spark of interest when I told her about the delivery to the Darkwaiths' flat.

"Yes, gone. Which means somebody is inside flat 228 right now. The box was there, and then it was gone. *Someone* took it inside."

"That is interesting," Minerva said, but her tone was lukewarm.

I put my napkin down beside my plate. "Shall we talk about what's disturbed you?"

"I'm sorry. I've been a poor hostess."

"Not at all. The curry was delicious, and you held up your end of conversation for most of the evening, but it's as if there's a film preventing you from fully engaging tonight." I propped my elbow on the table and put my chin in my palm. "Tell me all about it. You so rarely have any issues. It will be nice to have the shoe on the other foot. Let *me* listen to *your* problem."

As fellow working girls, we'd become good friends quickly. I suspected Minerva was a few years older than me. She was certainly further along in her career. She'd established herself as a successful cartoonist and lived independently. She'd eased my transition into South Regent Mansions, introducing me to the fellow residents on our floor. She'd given me hints about which shops nearby stocked high-quality goods. She'd also warned it was best to avoid the prickly Mrs. Attenborough if possible. Now it seemed I might be able to return the favor and help her.

Minerva ran her fingers through her short, light brown curls, disarranging them. I noticed a smudge of ink on the back of her hand, more evidence that something was definitely off. She was always perfectly turned out whether she was going into the newspaper office in one of her severe outfits or simply drawing at her desk at home.

She refilled both of our glasses. "I warn you, this is going to sound as if I'm mad."

"Try me. I've heard some pretty incredible stories."

CHAPTER THREE

*M*inerva leaned back in her chair and focused on the chandelier, seeming to gather her thoughts, then her gaze dropped to me. "I had to go down to Fleet Street today. I was running late and flew out of here and raced along the hall to the lift." Her recitation of these events had been matter-of-fact, but now the pace of her words slowed. "It was when I was in the lift going down that I saw something"—she took a gulp of wine, then carefully set down her glass—"a carpet, rolled up and leaning against the doorframe of two twenty-three."

Her narrative halted, and after a few seconds of silence, I said, "The Kemps' flat. Yes, I saw it too when I left the building earlier today. I thought what a dreadful day to move house with the drizzle and cold."

She had been rotating the stem of her wineglass, but her hand froze. "You saw the rug?"

"Yes."

Her gaze fixed on me with an intensity that indicated she was noting every subtle change in my expression. "And did you notice anything . . . unusual?"

My answer obviously mattered a great deal to her. "No," I said slowly.

Disappointment flashed over Minerva's face. "Nothing strange at all?"

"Well, I did think it was a bit odd that the door to 223 was closed and the movers had left the carpet propped up in the hall. But I supposed they were on their lunch break and would be back for it later."

Minerva, her voice preoccupied, said, "Yes, it was awfully quiet in the hallway when I left as well, now that I think about it. Did you see anyone else about?"

Worry curled through me. I'd thought she had some domestic issue troubling her—some minor contretemps with a neighbor that we could sort out over pudding—but this was something beyond that. What had rattled someone as imperturbable as Minerva?

"No one was about, except the maid, of course," I said. "She'd finished with my flat. I followed her out as she left to go next door to Lola and Constance's flat."

Minerva nodded and let out a sigh that signaled dissatisfaction as she swept her hair off her forehead, mussing her curls even more. "There's really no way to tell you, except to come out and say it." She crossed her arms and braced them on the table as she leaned forward. "I wasn't really paying attention—I wish I had been! I was thinking about how fine I was cutting it on time, and I almost missed it."

"Almost missed what?"

"As the lift descended, my gaze traveled down the length of the rolled-up rug. Something was sticking out of the bottom of it. I only caught a glimpse of it before my view was cut off as the lift went down."

"What was it? What did you see?"

"A foot."

I blinked. "A foot? Are you sure?"

"Yes." Misery filled every ounce of the single syllable. "I've spent all day attempting to talk myself out of it, but I'm completely and utterly sure."

"Of course you are." If Minerva said she'd seen a foot, then she'd seen a foot. She wasn't prone to flights of fancy. "Oh my."

"Yes." She reached for her wineglass but didn't pick it up, only ran her hand up and down the stem. "I spent all afternoon dwelling on it. In that first moment, I did think I was mistaken—how could I *not* be mistaken? A foot? But you know how slow the lift is. I definitely had time to see it and process what it was—" She shook her head, a tiny little motion, as she shrugged. "I just couldn't believe it. It was too bizarre. But it *was* a foot."

"No shoe?"

"No. Just a bare foot. I couldn't tell you if it was a man or woman's, but it was a human foot, and it had a slightly bluish tinge to it."

"Oh." I swallowed and looked away from the food left on my plate. "What did you do?"

"I was so stunned that for a moment I didn't know what to do. Then, of course, I had to go back up."

"Of course."

"But it seemed to take forever. You know how the lift creeps along. An older lady on the first floor was waiting, so the lift stopped there. Once she'd stepped out into the lobby, I hit the button for the second floor. But by the time the lift heaved itself up to it again, the carpet was gone."

CHAPTER FOUR

"The carpet was gone? Goodness! What did you do?" I asked Minerva.

"I told myself that I'd misinterpreted what I'd seen. It couldn't possibly have been a human foot." She drained the last of the wine out of her glass and put it down, her attention focused on setting it exactly into the faint circular imprint on the tablecloth. With her head tilted down, she looked up at me and held my gaze. "I played the coward. I should have asked the porter to come up and search for it right away. I should have insisted, even if it caused a horrible scene." Her gaze dropped. "But I didn't. I told myself that if I was late for the meeting at the paper, I wouldn't have a job tomorrow."

"From what you've said about your boss, that sounds like an accurate assessment."

The corners of Minerva's mouth turned up in a brief smile. "Yes, that's true. Old Harrison is looking for any excuse to get rid of me. He's still angry his chum didn't get my job."

She pushed her hair off her forehead again, disarranging it even more. "But the fact remains that I *did* see a foot. Despite trying to convince myself all afternoon that I didn't, I know what I saw. It was a foot, therefore there was a body wrapped in the carpet. The foot had a definite bluish hue, therefore the logical conclusion is that there was a *dead* body in the carpet. The next reasonable deduction is that it must be murder. Otherwise, why would a body be wrapped in a carpet? There can't be any other reason for that."

"Excellent logic—and all rather ominous signs. What a horrific experience. Do you want me to stay with you while you speak to the police?"

"I can't." She sat up straight.

Thinking that she was nervous about speaking to the officials, I said, "I'm sure it will be fine."

"No, it won't."

"Come on, Minerva, buck up. Where's that girl who marched into the editor's office at *The Hullabaloo* with her portfolio and made him take a look at it? Speaking to the police won't be nearly as nerve-racking as that." When I'd first met her, I'd coaxed Minerva into telling me how she'd landed a job as a cartoonist with one of the London papers —not an easy feat for a woman to achieve.

She gave a sharp shake of her head. "That was different. I was after a job then, not proclaiming there'd been a murder. There's a time to be bold and move forward decisively, and there's a time to lie low and not draw attention to oneself, Olive. *This* is definitely a time to lie low. Besides, now that old Harrison is my boss, I almost wish I hadn't been so bold."

"But if there was a dead body, you must—"

"As I said, I can't." Her perfect posture emphasized her firm tone. "If I contact the police, inquiries will be made. If word gets back to Harrison—if there's even a *hint* that I was involved with something scandalous . . . well, that would be it for me at the paper." She lashed her hand through the air in a sweeping motion. "I'd be out."

"But why would Harrison ever know? The police inquiries would focus on South Regent Mansions."

Minerva shifted in her chair, angling her body so she faced me directly. "I've already spent hours mulling over it, Olive. Obviously, something horrible happened here on the second floor. Equally apparent is the fact that someone is desperate to keep it quiet. You don't really believe that if the police come here and begin asking questions that someone will say, 'Oh yes, I rolled the body up in the carpet and left it in the hall for a few moments. That was me.'"

"Yes, you're right." I had a sinking sensation in my stomach. I knew what was coming.

"You've never said much about the cases you've worked on, but I read the paper. People will do anything to keep their secrets. If the police begin asking questions and there's not a clear answer about who decided a rug was a good place to store a dead body, then attention will shift to me. You know how things will go, Olive. They'll think I'm mad. I can't have a hint of that. I won't be branded as barmy. I can't be. If it were just me, it would be different. But Mummy depends on me."

I hadn't met Minerva's mother, who lived in a cottage in Somerset. Minerva visited her often but didn't speak about her much. All I'd gathered was that her mother had palsy, and that her health had gone downhill rapidly a few years ago.

"You know if there's the slightest whisper of me being imbalanced, Harrison will use that to oust me. That's why need you. I want you to find out who was in the carpet, *then* we'll contact the police." She began to stack the dishes.

I didn't miss the subtle shift to the plural pronoun. I decided to let that go for the moment and focus on the main point. "I do see why you'd want to approach the situation that way, but the police frown on that sort of thing—poking around in a possible murder inquiry. In fact, you'd appear even more suspicious because you waited."

Minerva pushed back her chair and picked up our plates. "I'm aware of that, but it's irrelevant now. I didn't contact them immediately. Whether I wait a few hours or a few days, it all works out the same. I still delayed. Since I put it off, we might as well make use of the time. Besides, if we can present them with truth instead of questions, it will be much better in the long run. I have to protect myself. I was cautious and guarded earlier today, so discovering what happened before we approach the police is the route that we must take." I made a move to rise and help her with the dishes, but she waved me off. "The kitchen is too small for more than one person. I'll bring back the pudding, then you can continue your objections to my plan," she added with a faint smile.

Dishes clattered and water ran while I contemplated

Minerva's points. As much as I disliked the situation, I could see why she didn't want to go to the police. She was right. The time to do that had been earlier. The delay would raise questions. I brushed a few crumbs from the table and tried to push away the unease that I felt for her. She should have gone to the police, but since she hadn't . . . As my mother had often said, it was no use looking back. Better to press ahead.

The rich scent of freshly brewed coffee filled the flat, and Minerva returned a few minutes later carrying a tray with plates of strawberries and ice cream as well as two cups of coffee. Once she'd distributed the food, she picked up her fork. "Well? Now that you've had a few moments, what do you think?"

"It's a very distressing situation, and I do understand your hesitancy to go to the police."

"Then you'll help me?"

"Yes, of course." Even though I'd only known her a few months, she was my friend. She was in a bad spot, and I couldn't let her down.

She breathed out. "Thank you, Olive. I'll pay your going rate—"

I held up a hand to stop her words. "I couldn't charge you."

"Oh yes, you will. I need your expertise. I'm as thrifty as the next person when I need to be, but I've learned that there are times when it's worth it to pay for the best. When it comes to handling delicate situations—and this is a delicate situation if there ever was one—I need the best, and that's you, Olive."

"You're too kind—"

"Nonsense. It's the truth." She jumped up and retrieved a sketchbook from the sideboard. "Now, I made a list." She flipped past sketches until she came to a page with a list of names. She handed the book to me. "We just have to figure out who's missing, and then we'll know who was wrapped up in the carpet. That can't be too difficult, can it? After all, there's only a handful of flats on this floor."

I pushed away my plate. Talking of dead bodies rolled up in carpets tended to put one's appetite off.

"This is a starting point," I said as I scanned down the list of residents of the second floor. "But I think we should go back a bit. Did you notice anything else about the foot besides the faint blue color? Was it large or small? Did it look like a man or woman's foot?"

"It was a just a glimpse. It wasn't tiny or overly large, so I suppose if I had to pick a size, I'd say it was medium, but it happened so fast that I didn't take in any extra details about it."

"Okay, what about the rug?"

Minerva closed her eyes for a moment, then they popped opened. "It wasn't fringed. I do remember that."

"That's good. Color?"

"I saw the underside of it, so I couldn't tell you much about the pattern, but it was brown and something darker— maybe black or blue."

"Excellent. Anything else?"

She frowned at her plate and speared a strawberry in an idle way, then swished it through the melting ice cream. "No, that's all. I know it's not much."

"It's a start, but there's something else we have to consider. What if whoever was in the carpet was someone who was visiting South Regent Mansions? What if they weren't a resident?"

Minerva put her fork down. "I hadn't thought of that, but I suppose we have to consider it."

"We do, which means the possibilities aren't limited to only the residents of the second floor."

"All right, then." Minerva squared her shoulders. "The porter will know if anyone had a visitor this morning. I'll talk to him and find out what the comings and goings were today."

"That's a good idea. We'll have to add any visitors to this list." I frowned. "But this list is too short. We can't limit ourselves to just the people on the second floor. It could be anyone in the building." I held the sketchbook out to her. "This is too big, Minerva. I'm sorry. I thought I could help, but it's beyond what I can do." She didn't take it. Instead, she drew a breath, but I cut off the protest I knew was coming. "Truly, it is. We can't possibly check on the whereabouts of everyone in this building. How many people live here? Hundreds, at least." I put the sketchbook down on the table.

Minerva's shoulders sagged, and I knew she was thinking of floor after floor of flats. The new electric panel in the lift had twenty buttons and each floor had ten flats, but each flat could have multiple occupants. Minerva spun the sketchbook so she could look at the list. "And that's why I asked for your help." She blew out a sigh. "You see things that I can't. It was a bit naive of me to not see how wide the possibilities were. I never even thought about it being anyone besides someone from our floor."

She half-closed the book, then stopped. "Hold on. It may have been some stranger who was visiting or a resident of another floor, but isn't it *most likely* that the body I saw in the carpet was someone from this floor?" She didn't wait for me to answer but rushed on, her words coming quickly. "I mean, if you have a body rolled up in a rug, it would make sense that you wouldn't want to move it any farther than you had to, right? Dead bodies are heavy, aren't they?"

"Not having personal experience in that area, I can only guess, but I imagine you're correct."

Minerva inched forward in her chair and tapped the list. "Then it's most likely that the body was one of these people. If you live on, say, the tenth floor and go to all the effort to roll a dead body in a carpet, why would you drag it down to the second floor, then go off and abandon it?"

"Lots of reasons," I said. "Misdirection, for one. Because you saw the body on the second floor, you assumed it came from this floor. That's exactly why someone—the murderer—would move the body to another floor."

"But think of the risk! Anyone might see you as you moved it. I know if I saw someone dragging a bulky carpet either into the lift, or worse, up or down the stairs—" Minerva's hooded eyes widened. "Oh! The repairman! It *must* have been someone on this floor. I know it."

I realized what she meant. "That's right. The repairman worked on the lift this morning. I had to take the stairs earlier when I left the building at half past noon because he was working on the lift."

"It was fixed when I left about fifteen minutes after that," Minerva said. "I was running late and checked the time as I walked out the door. It was twelve forty-four."

"We'll need to find out exactly when the repairman left," I said.

"Evans will know. He'll have it logged in his ledger."

"Yes, he will." Evans manned the alcove inside the lobby, handling mail and deliveries as well as keeping the log of activity in a thick ledger that was always open in front of him.

"I'll think of some excuse to ask him for the details," Minerva said. "So, this is good, right? It narrows down the time that someone could have moved the body using the lift."

"That's true, but there's still the back stairs—" I'd been using a measured tone, trying to tamp down Minerva's enthusiasm, but I broke off.

Minerva bounced a little and leaned forward. "The painters!"

"That's right. They were here today, weren't they?"

Minerva nodded, her disarranged fringe fluttering around her arched eyebrows. "Yes, working their way down from the top floor." Minerva hopped up, opened a drawer in the sideboard, and took out a sheet of paper that I recognized. I'd received the same letter. "Here it is." She read from the page, "'Painting to begin Monday week. Back stairs to be inaccessible. Management apologizes for the inconvenience.'"

Minerva strode to her desk, snatched up a pencil, and returned to the table. She turned to a new page in the sketchbook and bent over as she wrote. "That's another thing to ask Evans. I'll find out exactly what time the repairman left and how long the painters worked, but I think that makes it even more likely it was someone on this floor. If you're going to go to the trouble to move a body that's rolled up in a carpet, you certainly wouldn't want to carry it down a staircase that might be occupied with workmen."

"Not to mention freshly painted walls," I said. "But didn't you say the hallway was very quiet when you left to go to the office?"

"The painters must have been on their lunch break. The door was propped open for ventilation. Fumes, you know. I didn't hear any sounds—no voices or movement—nothing at all." Minerva shifted forward so that she was perched on the edge of her chair. "Discovering who was in the rug isn't such an overwhelming task. I can tell you still have reservations, but will you please just help me sort out if anyone is missing on this floor? It shouldn't be that difficult. It's only ten people instead of hundreds—and that's including both of the Kemps."

South Regent Mansions had a sister building, North Regent Mansions, and the numbering scheme for the buildings was unique. Flats on each floor in the north building were numbered from ten to nineteen, with the floor number as a prefix. Flats in the south building were numbered from twenty to twenty-nine, with the floor number as a prefix. So, the ten flats on the second floor of South Regent Mansions were numbered from 220 to 229. Apparently, the builder thought that higher numbers conveyed a more exclusive atmosphere. It also meant that letters were rarely delivered to the wrong building.

"Well, not even that many, actually. I saw Mrs. Attenborough on my way in today, and I chatted briefly with Lola when I popped out to get the wine."

"Excellent." Minerva drew lines through their names. "And I had the note tonight from Mr. Culpepper. We can mark him off as well. Only seven to go."

$\mathcal{T}$he next morning, I sat at my typewriter banging out my report, trying to keep my eyes on my notebook, not on the typewriter keys. I'd been practicing faithfully, following Jasper's advice. He was an excellent touch typist—a product of his years in the Admiralty during the war—and he'd told me the only way to become a speedy typist was to practice. "One must resolve not to look at the typewriter," he'd said. "Otherwise, one ends up using the two-finger hunt-and-peck method."

I'd been practicing each evening, but my skills were sadly below the level of Jasper's expertise. However, after three attempts, I had managed to produce an error-free summary of my investigation for Lola. I pulled it from the platen with a sense of satisfaction. I placed it in a folder and set it aside. I would take it to her that afternoon when I went to tea.

By the time Minerva and I had finished dinner last evening and created a strategy to check on each person on the second floor, it had been quite late—far too late to concoct an excuse to knock on every door, which would have been the opposite of the discreet inquiry Minerva wanted. It hadn't been too late to investigate the uninhabited parts of South Regent Mansions, though.

We'd taken torches and crept about the top floor. It hadn't taken us long to confirm that the rug or a blue-tinged foot connected to a dead body wasn't in the attic. A layer of dust over the floorboards confirmed that no one had been in the attics recently. Leftover molding and floor tiles were stacked in a corner along with a cracked light fixture. Boxes and several pieces of luggage, including my trunk, stood arranged in aisles across the center of the space, each labeled with a flat number. None of them were large enough to hold a body. We were able to easily shift the larger ones, so they had to be empty. The few that were heavy were too small to be of interest to us. There wasn't a single rolled carpet among the items stored in the attic either. We'd taken the stairs down to the basement and found even less of interest to us there. It was a small, dark space with bins for removing the rubbish and little else. Since it had been too late to begin our inquiries about the second-floor residents that evening, we'd returned to our flats with a plan to begin our investigation the next morning.

Minerva had to go to Fleet Street that morning, and I had to keep an appointment that I'd scheduled the previous week in order to complete my project for Lola. A few weeks ago, I'd had a note from Lola asking if I could meet her for tea at a nearby Lyon's. Over tea and toast, she'd described a simple job. Lola wanted me to look over the financial records of two charities and assure her that they were actually helping people with the money they'd received. I'd suggested an accountant, but she'd said, "Your father was a vicar?"

I'd nodded, not sure where the conversation was headed.

"And did you help him with the parish books?"

"Well, yes. He's rather absentminded and tended to overlook the more mundane things like accountancy."

She nodded. "I thought that might be the case. You're the perfect person to examine the books of two religious charities. I'd rather not deal with an accountant." She wrinkled her nose. "I'm not fond of the species. And I'd rather the charities not know of my interest. It saves a lot of tedious questions and pestering later."

I assumed that Lola intended to make a donation to one or possibly both and wanted to make sure her money would be put to good use. I'd accepted the job and used my connections in high society to complete the commission. A former client of mine, Lady Mulvern, was involved in one of the charities, and she'd paved the way for me with that charity last week.

Then I'd rung up the mother of an old school chum who was a society matron and a member of the other charity's board. Once I explained I was making discreet inquiries on the behalf of a possible donor who wanted to remain anonymous, she'd arranged for me to speak with the charity's treasurer, who was more than happy to let me look over the books.

It hadn't taken long that morning to confirm that the

charity, a soup kitchen run by a church, was legitimate and doing excellent work to help the poor. I hadn't thought that my investigation would reveal any surprises, but Lola had hired me to make inquiries, so inquiries had been made. I'd be able to give her a full report that afternoon when I met with her at teatime.

As I was fastening the cover over the typewriter, a faint whooshing sound came from the hallway. I snapped the cover into place and went to investigate.

A white piece of paper lay on the carpet. It was a page of notepaper that had been folded and pushed through the gap between the bottom of my door and the threshold.

Dear Miss Belgrave,

Lola received a telegram from a relative and has been called away. She asked that I send you this note with her regrets. She cannot meet for tea this afternoon. She will return on Wednesday and will be happy to see you that afternoon, if that is acceptable.

Sincerely,
Constance Duskin

I folded the note and tapped it against my palm. It struck me as a bit odd that Lola had asked Constance to write to me, despite the fact that the two women shared a flat.

The roommates were both fair and about the same

height, but one would never mistake them. Lola was slender and had flaxen hair, which she wore swept back from her forehead. She had ivory skin, an upturned nose, and a heart-shaped face. Constance's hair was a darker blonde, and she had a fringe that nearly covered her straight eyebrows. Her face was more rounded, her figure was fuller, and she moved with a heavy stride. Perhaps it was Lola's favorite pale green coat the color of willow leaves in the spring that prompted the association, but Lola brought to mind a willow tree with its thin, swaying branches, while Constance, in her unchanging wardrobe of brown and black, was more like a sturdy oak.

When I'd first met the two women, I'd thought Lola was timid. The few times I'd encountered them together, it seemed Lola was happy to defer to Constance, who had a strong personality. I'd met both women at Minerva's dinner party, where I'd been partnered with Mr. Culpepper. It had been Constance who did most of the talking, often answering questions directed at Lola. Constance had even refused pudding for both of them, saying they were reducing.

"Poor Lola," Minerva had said as we cleared the table after the two women left. "Imagine living with someone who's so pushy. I wonder if Constance dictates their break-fast menu as well."

But when Lola hired me and I'd met with her one-on-one, it was apparent that Lola knew exactly what she wanted. I'd revised my opinion of her after that meeting. Lola wasn't cowed. She was simply easygoing. She let Constance run things—or perhaps the more accurate statement was that Lola let Constance have a free hand in the things that didn't matter to her. Apparently pudding fell into that category. I wouldn't be so laconic when it came to sweets—they were a weakness of mine—but then again, Constance worked in a department store. She had to look smart and keep her figure. Perhaps Lola had been supporting Constance by not having dessert.

I refolded the note from Constance and put it on my desk with the finished report for Lola. She had one stipulation for my assignment—that I not speak to anyone else about it except her. I didn't know why she'd added this requirement, but I'd had clients make unusual requests before. I couldn't see any way that the request would be harmful, so I'd agreed and gone about the job.

The fact that Lola had informed Constance that I was coming to tea and asked her to write the note indicated that something unexpected had indeed come up. I went to my desk and penned a note saying that I would be free Wednesday afternoon and would be delighted to see Lola then. I sealed it in an envelope and put it beside my handbag.

Constance worked as a salesclerk at a Montford's Department Store and wouldn't be home at that time of the day. She must have dropped the note off on her way to work, so I'd do the same and slide the message under the door to flat 225.

I turned my attention to the list Minerva and I had made the previous evening. We'd divvied up the residents of the second floor. Minerva would get in touch with Diana Finch-Ellis and check with Evans about the workmen who'd been in and out of the building. She'd also ask Evans where the Kemps had moved. I was to check on Mr. Popinjay and Miss Bobbin. Minerva had seen Miss Bobbin in the lift the day prior to the dinner party. She'd said she was feeling under the weather and wouldn't attend, but since that had been Sunday, the day before Minerva saw the carpet, we had to check on Miss Bobbin.

I picked up a pencil to cross the name *Constance* off the list, but then I hesitated. I only had a note. I didn't know Constance's handwriting. Anyone could have written that note and shoved it under my door. I put the pencil down. I would wait until I'd actually spoken to her before marking her name off the list.

I went to fetch my hat and coat. Miss Bobbin walked her dog in the park every day about this time.

CHAPTER SIX

*I*t should have been easy to find Miss Bobbin in the park across the street from South Regent Mansions. Despite being in her sixth—or perhaps seventh—decade, she had jet black hair, and she was nearly as slender as one of the wrought-iron palings in the fence that surrounded the park where she walked her wire fox terrier, Ace, every day. But I'd made a complete circuit of the oval park, even looking behind the dense band of shrubbery at the far end, and hadn't seen Miss Bobbin.

As I returned along the gravel walk to the gate, a somber sensation settled on me. I'd expected to spot Miss Bobbin right away. The longer I went without seeing her, my twinge of worry grew stronger.

I wrapped my scarf tighter around my neck as a sharp gust cut across my face. A stiff wind had cleared out the fog, and a sapphire-blue sky showed through the bare branches of the chestnut trees. I came out of the park and spotted Miss Bobbin's angular figure. Her bulky coat didn't disguise her sharp elbows and rail-like shoulders. She was walking at a good clip toward me as she made her way along the street that ran between the mansion block and the park.

Relief spiked through me, which surprised me. Miss Bobbin was a spinster and lived alone, but she wasn't one of those comfortably plump older women one associates with knitting and freshly baked scones. Miss Bobbin certainly didn't bring to mind gooey baked goods. No, she was more tart than sweet. Her affectionate dog, Ace, made up for her rather standoffish demeanor. He skimmed along the pavement at the very maximum point that the lead would extend. He always greeted me with unrestrained joy when we happened to meet.

I timed my crossing so that I joined them as they reached the door to the lobby. "Hello, Miss Bobbin." She paused to let me pet Ace, who was quivering in delight as I greeted him with an ear rub. "Are you feeling better? Minerva said you were a bit under the weather last evening."

"Hello, Miss Belgrave. Yes, thank you. The chilly weather was the culprit, I believe. Sunshine does wonders for one, doesn't it?"

We walked the length of the lobby's scarlet runner with Ace crisscrossing our path in excitement. "Today is quite an improvement over yesterday," I said as we entered the lift and I closed the gate.

"Indeed. Quite lovely for February. Ace wanted to go farther than the park today, so I had to indulge him."

Ace had his nose pressed to the seam where the gate met the frame of the lift, poised so that he could dash out the moment we reached the second floor. At the sound of his name, he twisted his head back to look at Miss Bobbin. Her sharp features softened as she smiled at the dog.

Miss Bobbin turned her attention back to me. "We've had quite a lot of excitement here at the Mansions, haven't we?"

"Have we?" I asked. I tried to keep the wariness out of my tone, but I wasn't completely successful. Was she hinting she knew something about the rolled-up carpet?

"Yesterday, with the movers in, the repairman, and the painters as well."

"Oh. Yes. Right. Of course. It has been busy lately." If that statement had come from Mrs. Attenborough, it would have been shot through with disapproval, but Miss Bobbin didn't seem to mind the invasion of workmen.

"Poor Ace. He's exhausted from constantly monitoring the noises coming from the hallway. He was on alert all day yesterday."

"I don't suppose you know where the Kemps have moved?"

"No, I'm afraid not."

"You didn't happen to notice anything . . . unusual in the hallway yesterday? I mean, apart from all the workmen."

"No, I stayed in. Because of my sniffle, you know. Evans was kind enough to take Ace to the park for me, so I didn't have to go out at all."

"That was nice of Evans. I'd be happy to walk Ace if you don't feel like going out."

"Thank you. I'll keep that in mind," she said, but I imagined she'd only ask as an absolute last resort. She seemed

like the sort who'd rather not depend on—or be beholden to
—anyone.

As the lift surged to its bouncy stop, a thought occurred
to me. "How long have you lived in South Regent Mansions,
Miss Bobbin?"

"Since the year it opened."

"So, you've seen lots of people come and go."

"Oh yes."

Ace, excited about dashing out of the lift, circled around
the lift, then returned to the gate, looping the lead around
my ankles.

As I extracted myself, I asked, "Have you ever met the
current residents of number two twenty-eight?"

"No, they tend to keep to themselves. In fact, I only
know the name. It's on the residence roster, you know. I did
send them an invitation to one of my bridge evenings, but
they politely declined. Do you play bridge, Miss Belgrave?"

"Yes, I do."

"Then I'll send you an invitation to my next bridge
party."

"I look forward to it." I unlatched the gate. Ace shot
forward, and Miss Bobbin stepped quickly, keeping up with
the zippy pace the dog set. "Care for a cup of tea, Miss
Belgrave?" she asked over her shoulder.

"Yes, thank you."

The door to flat 220 at the end of the hallway opened an
inch. A ginger-colored cat melted through the small gap and
flashed down the hall's scarlet runner. Miss Bobbin must
have relaxed her grip on the lead, because Ace darted away
after the cat, lead trailing along the floor. Chaos reigned in

the passageway as the cat and dog streaked up and down the runner, bumping against the occasional tables that lined the hall. Miss Bobbin lunged for Ace's lead, and I darted back and forth, steadying the vases of flowers on the tables that the animals had set rocking.

Mr. Popinjay emerged from flat 220 and joined the race up and down the hall. Even though he was squat and of a rather rotund build, he was agile. He managed to scoop up the cat and press the squirming creature to his rounded stomach. One of the cat's paws hit his bowtie and knocked it askew, but he didn't notice. "That dog is a menace!" he shouted as he returned to his flat. "It frightens Desdemona. She might have been injured."

Miss Bobbin straightened her hat. "Ace isn't a menace. He was perfectly behaved until your animal raced through the building, colliding with the furniture and causing a disturbance. You can't expect a dog *not* to chase a cat."

Mr. Popinjay slammed his door, but Miss Bobbin carried on. "It goes against the very nature of a dog."

The lock on the door of flat 220 clicked into place.

Miss Bobbin let out a huff. "That *man* is a menace," she announced to the hallway, then she marched to her flat, 222, and closed the door with a thud.

"Well, it seems I'm making my own tea today." I returned to my flat and marked the names of Miss Bobbin and Mr. Popinjay off my list.

I'd just sat down with a cup of tea—which I'd made for myself—and my list of names when a knock reverberated through the flat.

I thought it might be Miss Bobbin returning to apologize for forgetting about her invitation to tea, but it was Minerva who stood on the threshold. "I have news," she announced.

"So do I. Come in. Cup of tea?"

"Yes, please. I need one."

"Something wrong at the newspaper office?"

"No, it's exactly the same there. Old Harrison is as unhappy with me as ever. I have drawings that I must complete this afternoon, but I'm feeling a bit frazzled. I'm afraid I won't be able to settle."

I came out of the kitchen with a new cup and saucer and motioned for her to follow me into the sitting room. "After your experience yesterday, it's no wonder you feel that way. What's your news?" I poured the tea.

She handed me a crumpled piece of paper from her pocket. "I have the address for the Kemps."

"Excellent. Where is it?" I asked as I jotted it down on the list of names.

"Bloomsbury."

"All right, I'll go by there this afternoon."

"I've already gone. I spoke to Evans this morning on my way to Fleet Street. I made up a story about having to return something to Mrs. Kemp to get their new address. As soon as I finished at Fleet Street, I went to Islington. I saw both Mr. and Mrs. Kemp."

"Oh, did you speak to them?"

She shook her head as a small smile flickered across her bright red lips. "That would have been awkward, don't you think? Especially since I don't actually have anything to return to them. I couldn't think of a good reason that I'd pop over to their new address. I hovered on the corner, consulting a piece of paper as if I were lost. They were returning from some sort of errand. They went into a terraced flat."

"That's good. We can mark them off our list."

Minerva took a sip of her tea and returned it to her saucer. "I also have the times the workmen were here and when they left."

"Well done."

"I was quite chatty with Evans, and he was happy to let me look over the ledger. He keeps excellent records."

"Thank goodness. What were the timings of the workmen?" I asked, pen poised.

"Exactly what we thought. The lift repairman finished up at twelve thirty-five, and the painters took a break for lunch from twelve to one. And they also told Evans when they left for lunch that they'd finished the second-floor stairwell. When they returned from lunch, they said they'd do the rest of the stairwell and be out by about three o'clock."

I scribbled down the times, then Minerva asked, "You found out something as well?"

I put down my list and settled back in my chair with my teacup. "Yes, both Miss Bobbin and Mr. Popinjay are alive and well—as are their pets. There was quite a scuffle in the hallway only a few moments ago."

Minerva grinned. "Let me guess. Cat versus dog? The usual contretemps?"

"Got it in one. Mr. Popinjay's cat got out of his flat and streaked down the hallway. Of course Miss Bobbin's dog went after it. Utter pandemonium for a few moments. Fortunately, none of the decor was broken, but Mr. Popinjay and Miss Bobbin are both quite annoyed."

"At loggerheads as usual."

"Indeed. So that's those two sorted. I've had a note from Constance saying that Lola has been called away unexpectedly."

"Better and better. We're making progress." Minerva turned the list of names toward her and reached for my pen. "That means that we can mark them off as well."

"Not yet."

She halted, pen in the air. "What? Why not?"

"Because I don't know Constance's handwriting. Anyone could have written that note and slipped it under my door. I can't mark off Constance until I actually see her."

"Yes, I suppose that's the best way to go about it." Minerva's arched brows lowered. "Then that means we also need to check on Mr. Culpepper."

"But I thought you'd heard from him yesterday?"

"He sent a note around saying he had to work and wouldn't be able to make it. But it's the same as with Constance. I don't know Mr. Culpepper's handwriting. You're right—anyone could have sent it."

"What time did the note arrive?"

"It was with the afternoon post."

"So, after you'd seen the body in the rug?" I asked to make doubly sure.

"Yes. Evans handed it to me when I arrived back from Fleet Street that afternoon."

"Do you still have the envelope? We could check the postmark ..." I trailed off.

Minerva was shaking her head. "I threw it in the rubbish when I was clearing up before dinner yesterday. It's gone."

Every flat in the building had a rubbish lift in the kitchen that ran down to the basement. The bins were emptied and returned each morning, which meant that the note would have gone out with the morning's rubbish.

"Then we can't mark off Mr. Culpepper," I agreed.

Minerva nodded and put the pen down. "Do you realize what this means? If Mr. Culpepper truly did send that note and Constance wrote the note to you, then that's everyone." Her complexion had taken on a pasty hue. "It means I was wrong, that someone wasn't rolled up in that rug. Oh, Olive. What's wrong with me? Perhaps I am barmy."

"Nonsense," I said, making my voice as sharp and school-mistressy as possible. "Of all the people I know, you're the least barmy. You laid out a very logical plan last night, and we'll follow it to its conclusion. We'll search for each person before we make any assumptions."

Minerva rubbed her hand across her forehead, ruffling her fringe. "Yes, you're right. I'm a little frazzled."

"Completely understandable."

She still looked distraught, so I tapped a name on the paper. "And you're also forgetting Diana Finch-Ellis."

"Oh, that's right." Relief flooded Minerva's face, but she

immediately shook her head. "How awful of me—I was actually relieved for a moment to think I was right—that I wasn't imagining things. How much better it would be if I was completely mistaken—even if it does mean I'm mad."

"You're not mad. You're sensible and logical and a little shaken by this, which is completely understandable."

"What if it *is* Diana? That would be terrible. I can't believe I mentally skipped right over her name. I was so focused on the Kemps and your news that I completely forgot about her."

"She is out an awful lot. I rarely see her."

"Miss Bobbin seems to be the only one who hears her—at two in the morning!"

"Yes, very inconvenient to have a leading socialite as a neighbor," I said.

"Well, after an evening at the theater, someone must make omelets for the Bright Young People."

I was glad to see a trace of Minerva's good humor return. "I'll check on her this afternoon," Minerva said. "She should be awake soon." Diana's schedule of parties and social events meant she often returned in the early hours of the morning, and she wasn't usually seen in the halls of South Regent Mansions before noon.

"And there's another flat you overlooked . . ." I pointed to the last name on the list.

"That's right, the Darkwaiths."

"We have to discover who is in flat 228," I said. "Perhaps Evans can help us there?"

Minerva shrugged. "No idea. I've tried to wheedle information out of him about the Darkwaiths before, but he's always been extremely cagey."

"We may have to find out what his weaknesses are."

"That sounds rather underhanded."

"Investigation often requires a little deviousness."

CHAPTER SEVEN

*M*inerva put down her tea. "Let's not wait until tonight to speak to Mr. Culpepper. Let's ring him up now." She jumped up. "You don't mind if I use your telephone, do you?"

Since she was halfway across the room to my desk, I said, "Of course not. You know where he's employed?"

"I know the name. He mentioned it at the dinner party when I asked him what he did. It was an odd combination of words, and it stuck in my mind. I should be able to find it if you have a directory here."

"Middle drawer on the left."

She flipped through the pages. "Duck, Dade and . . . something else."

"What sort of company is that?"

"An accountancy firm."

I'd been turned away, refilling my teacup, but at her words I set the teapot down and turned to look over the back of the couch. "Accountancy? I thought he worked in a

57

scientific sort of company. The few times that I've spoken with him, he's talked about his inventions and interesting scientific breakthroughs. I confess that I didn't understand some of what he said, but I do know it had to do with science and mechanical gizmos. I did pick up that much."

Head bent, Minerva paged through the directory. "The mechanical things are his hobby. His job is in accountancy. I was surprised too. I asked him why he never spoke about it, and he said most people find accountancy is dead boring. People were more interested in the fiddling he did with mechanical things."

"It hardly sounded like fiddling to me. He seemed to be frightfully knowledgeable."

"I agree. But apparently the gadgets are a hobby, not his job."

She ran her finger down the columns of the directory. "Although, he did tell me that he planned to approach an investor if he could get his prototype to work. He doesn't have the funds to manufacture it on a large scale."

"That's interesting. It sounds as if he doesn't find accountancy completely satisfying."

"No, I don't believe he does. Ah, here it is." She reached for the telephone. "Duck, Dade, and Croft."

"I can see why that name would stick in your memory." I stirred a sugar cube into my tea as she put the call through.

"Mr. Culpepper, please . . . oh. Well, when will he be back?"

I turned and looked over the back of the couch again.

Minerva jerked her head up, her expressive face conveying surprise. "He's out of town? In Edinburgh. Oh, I hadn't realized . . . No. No message. I'll contact him later. When should I ring back?" Her troubled gaze caught mine as she closed the directory. "In a few days. I see." She ended the call and came slowly back across the room. The energy and enthusiasm she'd had a few minutes earlier was gone. "They say that he had to leave unexpectedly on an urgent matter. Why didn't he put that in his note?"

"Perhaps he didn't have time."

"Perhaps," she said, but her tone was infused with doubt. She sat down, absently smoothing her skirt. I offered to refill her teacup, but she shook her head. "I don't think I could drink anything right now."

I put down the teapot. "All we have to do is speak to Evans again. He'll know exactly what time Mr. Culpepper left."

"But that's just it. The person I spoke to at his office said Mr. Culpepper left directly from work."

"He didn't even return here to get a suitcase?"

"Apparently not. The receptionist did say that Mr. Culpepper has family in Edinburgh and makes the trip frequently."

"He doesn't have a Scottish accent, but I suppose a member of his extended family could live there. Or his family could have moved there recently. But it is decidedly odd that he wouldn't at least take a valise with him."

Minerva scrubbed her hand across her forehead. "We're not clearing anything up. It's only getting more convoluted." The carriage clock on the mantel chimed the hour, and Minerva sighed. "I have to finish a drawing for Harrison. My deadline is in a few hours."

"Then focus all your attention on that. Let me check on Diana—that's one thing we can do. And I have an idea about how we can find out more about Mr. Culpepper."

Once Minerva left, I sat down at the desk, found a card that I'd tucked away in a drawer, and rang up an antique shop.

A gravelly voice answered, and I said, "Hello, is that you, Boggs? It's Olive Belgrave."

"Miss Belgrave! Delighted to hear from you."

I'd become acquainted with Boggs when I was working on another case. Since then, I'd recruited him a few times to help me out with cases. He'd been quite useful in discovering information in arenas and social situations that were closed to me. My position as a young lady of the upper class opened certain doors, but it also meant other doors were shut tight against me. Boggs excelled in areas where I was limited. "I wasn't sure you'd be in. I thought I might have to leave a message for you."

"Sadly, my play has been cancelled, and I'm at loose ends at the moment. Perhaps I might be of service to you?"

The last time I'd seen Boggs, he'd been in full costume. "I'm sorry to hear about the play—you made a smashing pirate—but I do have something I need help with."

"Wonderful. I've dusted everything in the shop, and my next audition isn't until Monday."

"I need information about a Mr. Culpepper. He works at Duck, Dade, and er—, I'm not sure of the final name of the company. It's an accountancy firm here in London."

"Shouldn't be that difficult to find."

"Yes, my thought as well. I especially need to know if Mr. Culpepper has relatives in Edinburgh, and if he traveled to Scotland yesterday."

"Sure. Sure. Shouldn't be too hard."

I was confident Boggs would suss out the information. He had a way of blending into whatever environment he happened to find himself in—a result of his acting skills, I was sure. He also had a knack for gaining the confidence of those around him—or he paid handsomely for information. I wasn't sure which method he'd employ with the accountancy firm, but either was fine with me. We needed to know the facts about Mr. Culpepper quickly, and I was confident that Boggs could discover them. "Will our usual rate suffice?" I asked. "Plus any expenses incurred, of course."

"Couldn't ask for better, Miss Belgrave," he said. "I'll go visit their offices this afternoon. Should I send a note around later tonight?"

"Please do. Or you can ring me directly. Let me give you my new address and number." I paused to give him time to get a pen and paper.

After he jotted it down, he said, "New digs for you, then?"

"Yes. I've moved to South Regent Mansions."

He chuckled. "I always knew it wouldn't be long before you left the boarding house. I'll be in touch."

Diana Finch-Ellis lived in flat 224, next door to Miss Bobbin in 222. I knocked on Diana's door. A fusillade of barks sounded from Miss Bobbin's flat, but there wasn't a flutter of movement behind Diana's door. After a few moments, I knocked more firmly. Ace's barks, which had tapered off, resumed at full volume.

Everyone on the second floor knew Diana had a rather rowdy set of friends who caused quite a commotion whenever she brought them home. Miss Bobbin had the worst of it, and I didn't want to get on her bad side by continuing to make noise. I'd have to come back later when Miss Bobbin took Ace for his evening walk. As I turned away, Miss Bobbin's door opened, and she poked her head out. "Oh, Miss Belgrave, it's you." She held Ace in one arm, tucked up against her tiny waist. "I thought Diana had lost her key again. She always makes such a racket."

"Does that happen often?"

"More than you'd believe. I know having a latchkey is all the rage with you Bright Young People, but she doesn't seem able to keep up with hers." Miss Bobbin nodded toward a painting of a waterfall that hung on the wall between their doors. "Miss Finch-Ellis keeps an extra latchkey on top of the frame. But invariably she knocks the painting off the wall, which sets Ace off. And of course it always happens in the middle of the night. I've told her it would be much better to leave an extra key with Evans, but she says that's no fun at all."

"Well, it seems she's not home now."

"No, she wouldn't be. She's visiting a friend in the country."

"Is she?"

"Yes, she left yesterday. She said I'd have several days of peace and quiet." Miss Bobbin shook her head. "She really is incorrigible—quite cheeky—but she has such a winning way about her that I find myself forgiving her, even though I really should be quite upset with her."

"Did you actually see her leave?"

"No. It was about ten when I spoke to her—shockingly early for her to be about, you know. She could tell I was surprised to see her at that time. She said she was usually a terrible slug-a-bed, but she had a train to catch around one and some errand to run before she departed for the station."

"Did she say where she was going?"

"Let me think. It wasn't far." She looked over my shoulder at the painting, her gaze unfocused. "Something with the word *court*. Let me think a moment. No, I can't remember, but it will come to me." Her attention fastened on my face again. "Now, I must apologize to you, Miss Belgrave. I completely forgot earlier today that I'd offered you tea. What with that horrible feline, my invitation completely went out of my mind. Would you like some now? Perhaps Miss Finch-Ellis' destination will come to me. It seems to be something you're keen to know."

"Oh, it's just that I need to speak to her, and I didn't realize she wouldn't be in town." I'd already had several cups of tea today, but if I could find out where Diana was, I'd drink another. "Yes, I have time for a cup of tea."

I followed Miss Bobbin into her flat. She set Ace down, and he greeted me like I was a long-lost member of the family. Miss Bobbin went to make tea, and I went into her sitting room with Ace circling around me, his tail swinging back and forth at a quick pace.

I hadn't been to one of Miss Bobbin's bridge parties, so I'd never seen the inside of her flat. Since she was a spinster, I imagined it would have been stuffed with bulky Victorian furniture with doilies scattered liberally about and knick-knacks wedged onto every flat surface, but it was quite the opposite.

Several modern landscapes hung on the walls, a few of them in the new Cubist style. The furnishings were stream-lined and modern, except for a button-backed Chesterfield sofa that was clearly Ace's domain. He jumped up and settled in one corner. Ferns and other potted plants were dotted around the room. Densely packed bookshelves lined one wall. Plaques and a couple of trophies ranged across the fireplace mantle. The one nearest to me was engraved with the words, *First Place, Sillbury Bridge Tournament, 1922.* On either side of the fireplace, the wall was covered with photographs of groups of school children in front of a three-story brick building. In each of the photos, off to the side of the children, I recognized the slender figure of a much younger Miss Bobbin standing in the line of teachers.

The clink of cutlery and china sounded, and I went to take the tray from Miss Bobbin. "Thank you, Miss Belgrave. Put it on the ottoman."

I positioned the tray, and she sat down on the sofa to pour for us.

I nodded to the mantel as I took a seat. "I was admiring your photographs. You were a teacher?"

"Head mathematics instructor at Dunbar School for Young Ladies."

"And you retired from there recently?"

"Yes, a few years ago. My niece and her husband found this flat for me, and I've lived here ever since."

"It's lovely."

"Thank you. After living in the quarters of the school my entire working life, it was delightful to shop for things for myself. I've enjoyed furnishing it. Some of my friends say it's too modern, but I rather like it."

"I do too."

She handed my tea over. "And I remember the name of the house where Miss Finch-Ellis went. It was Henley Court."

"I've heard of that. I believe it's in Surrey?"

"Yes, that's right. She was going down to Surrey, to Henley Court."

Ace had hopped down from the sofa and sat at attention in front of me. "But you didn't see her leave for the train?" I asked as I leaned over and stroked Ace's back.

"No, I only saw her in the morning."

"Oh."

Miss Bobbin tilted her head and looked a bit puzzled. "That's not the answer you wanted."

I smiled quickly to cover my slip. "No, it's fine. It just complicates things a bit." The fact that both Diana and Mr. Culpepper had left town the day before troubled me.

"What things?"

I pulled myself up. I'd almost launched into a summary of what I was about. She was an easy person to talk to, but I couldn't confide in her. Despite her cute dog and well-deco-rated flat, I didn't know Miss Bobbin at all. I had to take everything she said with a grain of salt. "Nothing impor-tant." I gave Ace a final pat and turned the conversation. "I noticed your bridge trophies."

"I have rather thrown myself into bridge. It's a nice way to meet people. I have an affinity for numbers, and I so enjoy a good trouncing of an opponent."

Ace trotted away and returned a few moments later with a ball between his teeth. He planted himself in front of my chair again and dropped the ball at my feet with an expec-tant look in his big brown eyes.

"Ace," Miss Bobbin said in a scolding tone, "leave our guest alone."

"It's fine." I put down my tea and tossed the ball for him. Ace raced after it, his legs flying across the room. "Did Miss Finch-Ellis say when she would return?"

"No, she didn't mention a specific day, only that I'd have a whole week of peace and quiet."

"Then I'll have to wait until then to speak to her. Earlier, you said you were surprised to see me in the hallway. Were you expecting to see someone else outside Miss Finch-Ellis' door?" Ace's legs pumped as he returned with the ball. I tossed it again.

"Oh no. Most of the time I don't know the people I see coming and going from her flat. Except, of course, for the young woman from flat 225. I believe her name is Miss Mallory?"

"Yes, that's right. Lola Mallory. I didn't realize she and Miss Finch-Ellis were friends."

A noise sounded from the hall. Ace cocked his head, ears perked, then dropped the ball and went off to give a few cursory barks and monitor the situation.

Miss Bobbin returned her cup to her saucer. "I'd hardly call their conversation friendly."

"Really? Why is that?"

"Well, I was returning from a walk with Ace, and I heard their raised voices. Of course, with Miss Finch-Ellis standing in her open doorway and Miss Mallory in the hallway, one can't help but overhear."

"Yes, that's true. I wonder what they were arguing about. They don't seem to be the sort who'd be well acquainted enough to have a disagreement." Glamorous and outgoing, Diana ran with a fast crowd, and photos of her continually popped up in the society columns. The few times I'd encountered her in the lobby, she'd breezed by in her mink, wafting expensive scent, her auburn hair always perfectly coiffed under a stylish hat. It didn't seem as if she'd have much in common with quiet, reticent Lola, who kept to herself.

"I don't know what they were discussing, but Miss Finch-Ellis looked extremely angry. I couldn't see Miss Mallory's expression, but she sounded earnest when she said it was only for Miss Finch-Ellis' own good, and that she —Miss Mallory, I mean—was only trying to help. Of course it was none of my business, so I merely nodded to both of them as I went into my flat."

"Yes, of course one would." I threw the ball for Ace a few more times, then thanked Miss Bobbin for the tea.

"You're welcome. I'll send you an invitation to my next bridge party."

"I look forward to it." I said the words automatically as I departed. I was already mentally making plans to call the local garage and ask for my Morris Cowley to be brought around as soon as possible. I suddenly felt the need to get out of the city. A drive along the country lanes was exactly what I needed, and Surrey would be the perfect destination.

CHAPTER EIGHT

a quarter of an hour later, I was motoring out of London, bundled in my wool coat and hat with my thickest scarf. The sky was patchy with clouds, and the air was chilly. Surrey wasn't far, and once I'd left London behind, the roads were perfectly passable, despite being sludgy along the edges from the recent rain.

I slowed as I approached the little village nearest Henley Court, then accelerated again once the cottages were behind me. Henley Court was an impressive Jacobean mansion. When I was a debutante, I'd attended a hunt ball there. It was situated in the hollow, and the road from the village rose up over the surrounding hills before dropping down to the valley where the estate was situated. If I remembered correctly, there was a section of the road at the peak of one of the hills that gave a perfect view of Henley Court nested in the trees.

I slowed as I spotted the viewing point and pulled the

Morris onto the berm, which was covered with gravel. Then I unsnapped the case that held my field glasses, which I now kept in my motor. I'd bought my father a pair of field glasses for Christmas. After discovering how useful they were, I'd returned to Harrods and purchased some for myself.

Smoke drifted from the chimneys, and the leaded-glass windows sparkled in the sunlight. A figure moved back and forth from the house to the outbuildings, but that was the only sign of movement. I waited a few more minutes with the field glasses trained on the mansion, but it appeared I wasn't going to be so lucky as to spot the members of the household out on a walk or returning from a ride.

As I wrapped the cord around my field glasses and returned them to their case, a Rolls Royce whipped by, and I caught a glimpse of a woman in the back seat. Reddish-brown curls peeked out from under her stylish cloche. Sunlight flashed, glancing off a jeweled clip, the hat's only decoration.

I tossed the field glass onto the seat and turned the wheel, taking the motor back onto the road. Diana Finch-Ellis' hair was that shade of auburn, and it was likely that the Rolls Royce belonged to the residents of Henley Court. Because I was facing the opposite direction, I had to drive about a quarter of a mile before I found a place to make a three-point turn between a gap in the hedgerows where a gate opened into pastureland.

The road wasn't busy, and I was able to catch up to the Rolls, but I kept my motor well back. The sleek sedan's speed dropped as it approached the nearby village, but the motor didn't stop there. I followed along, glad I'd asked the garage to fill my motor with petrol before they brought it around to South Regent Mansions. I had a can of petrol strapped onto the running board, and the garage attendant who'd delivered the Morris to my flat had said it was full, but if I had to stop to add petrol, the Rolls might be out of sight by the time I was back on the road.

The next community was a larger market town, and the Rolls pulled to a stop in front of one of the pubs. I drove on down the road, circled around the cenotaph, then inched the motor into the patchwork shade under the bare limbs of an old beech tree. I snagged my field glasses as the chauffeur moved smartly around the motor. Thankful there were no townspeople strolling along the road at that moment, I hunched low over the steering wheel and trained the field glasses on the passengers emerging from the Rolls.

Two women and two men climbed out and stood beside the sedan, scanning the shops, cottages, and the church. One of the women was Diana Finch-Ellis. I'd only passed her in the lobby and the hallway of South Regent Mansions, but she was memorable. There was no mistaking her shining hair or her tall and slender figure. She adjusted the lapels of her full-length mink as one of the young men with slicked-back dark hair and a carefree manner strolled over and offered his arm to her. His round face and fleshy lips looked familiar, but I couldn't bring his name to mind. The other two young people in the group had their backs to me. The four of them went into the pub.

I turned the motor in the direction of London. Diana Finch-Ellis was alive and well, visiting friends in the country. I was glad I'd have some good news to share with Minerva when I returned.

It was fully dark by the time I arrived back in the city. The roads were clogged with motorcars, delivery wagons, and pedestrians who darted across the streets, eager to get home after a day's work or shopping. I returned the Morris to the garage and planned to ask Minerva to join me for dinner if she was interested in dining on soup and sandwiches from the service flat's kitchen.

At South Regent Mansions, Evans' eggplant-shaped form blocked the door. A scruffy looking man in a worn tweed jacket and a droopy Homburg hat gestured inside the building, but Evans shook his head. The porter's deep voice carried across the pavement, "We have a policy about reporters at South Regent Mansions."

I trotted up the shallow steps, intending to slip past the two men and into the lobby.

The man asked, "What policy is that?"

"*No* reporters." Evans' tone was firm. The man in the tweed jacket backed up a step, and I saw his profile.

It was Boggs.

"Fine," the man said as he backtracked another few steps.

For a second, I considered approaching the men and smoothing things over. I was sure Boggs was there to visit me, but Evans was key to learning who had been in and out of the building. Part of his job was to defend the residents of South Regent Mansions from bothersome individuals such as reporters and salesmen. If Evans thought I was friendly with reporters . . . well, he'd be wary of me. I needed Evans on my side.

I halted and muttered, "Oh, bother. I forgot . . ." then pivoted and retreated down the steps. I set off at a brisk pace toward the shops at the end of the block. A few minutes later, Boggs fell into step beside me.

"So, you're a reporter now?" I asked.

"Amazing the number of doors that open when you mention the possibility of a favorable article in print."

"And is that what you promised Duck, Dade, and Croft?"

"In a way. They were very welcoming once I explained I was researching a piece on long-standing businesses situated in Westminster. The accountancy firm has been there since 1823."

Inwardly I cringed at the subterfuge, but I could see why Duck, Dade, and Croft had spoken to Boggs. "You certainly look the part of a newspaper man."

"Thank you. I was especially proud of the jacket. Bit scruffy, but still hanging onto the edge of respectability. Found it in a shop not long ago, and I've been saving it."

"Yes, it's ideal for the role, but it's more than the clothing. You somehow manage to change your manner as well."

When I first met Boggs, he had been the epitome of an upper-class servant, but now a cigarette dangled at the corner of his mouth as he strode along with a whirling gait, his arms swinging loosely at his sides. A well-thumbed notebook stuck out of one of his jacket pockets. He reminded me of the reporters who had descended on a small English village for the inquest after an unfortunate death at Archly Manor.

We crossed the street, dodging between a lorry and a taxi. "I try to get inside the person—to become them—for a few minutes, at least," Boggs said. "Today I've been a man on the hunt for a story."

"And your story was Mr. Culpepper?"

"Indeed. Initially, I asked plenty of questions about the firm of Duck, Dade, and Croft, but I did work my way around to their exemplary employees. Mr. Culpepper was at the top of the list."

"Really? I was under the impression that he did his work more as a means to an end rather than out of enjoyment."

"Whether he enjoys it or not, he's very good at what he does. So much so, that they sent him off to Edinburgh to meet with a rather finicky client."

"So, he *is* on a business trip?"

"Yes. Apparently, it's not the first time he's been dispatched to Edinburgh to meet with the client. Mr. Culpepper has a relative who lives in Edinburgh—a brother, they said. The firm often sends him to visit this rather prickly client whenever the client is in a snit. Sounds as if he's a cranky bugger—the client, I mean. He telephoned first thing Monday morning and demanded Duck, Dade, and Croft send someone right away. Mr. Culpepper traveled on the Flying Scotsman on Monday, First Class."

I waved to South Regent Mansions, which was visible ahead. "He didn't even return for luggage? Rather odd, that."

Boggs lifted a shoulder. "I agree and pressed the receptionist on that point and was told that Mr. Culpepper often visits his relative in Edinburgh and that he'd have every-thing he needed once he got there, so he didn't have to pack a bag."

"I suppose that could be the case, but I'd certainly want my own things."

"A man isn't so picky," Boggs said.

"Well, even if it's not how I'd travel, it's very helpful information." If Mr. Culpepper had taken the train that morning, he could have dropped a note in the post to Minerva before he left London.

Boggs pulled the notepad from his pocket and ripped a crinkled page from it as we made our way back toward the South Regent Mansions. He nodded toward the curved lines of the service flat, which rose up ahead of us, squares of golden light shining from the windows. "South Regent Mansions was on my way home, so I thought I'd drop this by instead of telephoning or mailing it. I didn't count on such a ferocious doorman."

"Evans is the head porter. He's very good at his job. Nothing gets past him."

"I'll say. I can usually wheedle my way into most places, but he was rather like a brick wall."

"As he should be. Residents don't want to be bothered by nosy reporters—except for me when *you* are the reporter."

He handed the page to me. "It's the address where Mr. Culpepper is staying in Edinburgh. I asked for it in case I had any follow-up questions."

"Brilliant work. Thank you. Although I do feel a bit sorry for Duck, Dade, and Croft. You didn't mention which paper you worked for, did you?"

"No. Said I was freelance, of course. But it could make a good article. Did you know that the firm employed one of the first women to become a chartered accountant? Called herself the 'lady accountant,' apparently. And that they've been in the same building since the firm was founded? And that the building was originally a guildhall for painters?"

"Interesting. You should contact Essie Matthews at *The Hullabaloo*."

"A friend of yours?"

"Yes. She writes a society column, but she's always on the lookout for a good story. She might be able to work it into one of her articles."

Boggs nodded. "I'll do that. But back to your bloke. Mr. Culpepper is due back in a few days."

"In a few days?"

My tone must have conveyed my despair at the news because Boggs said, "Need to speak to him urgently?"

"No, I only need to *see* him—or, at the very least, speak to him. Did you happen to get a telephone number?"

"The brother doesn't have one."

I sighed. "That makes it difficult. I need to know without a doubt that it was Mr. Culpepper who went to Edinburgh."

"But the office says he did."

"I know, but that's not good enough."

I felt Boggs look at me out of the corner of his eye. "Normally, I'd be happy to pop up to Scotland, but I have a commitment I can't avoid tomorrow."

"A new audition?"

"No, my mother's birthday."

"I couldn't ask you to miss that," I said. "And, besides, you don't know what Mr. Culpepper looks like."

We paced along in silence for a few strides. "Oh, it's like that, is it? Someone's missing?"

"Possibly. It looks as if I must make a trip to Edinburgh to find out if the individual is missing or not."

CHAPTER NINE

s soon as I reached the second floor of South Regent Mansions, I went directly to Minerva's door and knocked. I wasn't sure she'd be in, but after a few seconds, the door inched open and her face appeared in the gap. "Oh, it's you, Olive." The relief was palpable in her voice. She swung the door open. "Come in."

"What's wrong? Has something happened?"

Minerva shook her head and dismissed my concern with a dispirited wave of her hand. "I'm on edge, that's all. I'm expecting the police at any moment."

"You've spoken to them?"

She straightened as if I'd poked her in the ribs. "No. Of course not." She led the way into the sitting room. "I have an irrational fear that somehow they've found out about the body in the rug and are on their way to question me." She whirred one of her hands around in a circle. "It's just my thoughts going round and round. Here, let me tidy up."

Minerva picked up a large roll of paper and a sketchbook from the sofa cushions.

"Well, I have good news. I've seen Diana."

Minerva spun toward me, the paper and sketchbook dangling from her hands, forgotten. "You have?"

"Yes. She wasn't in her flat, but Diana told Miss Bobbin that she was going away to the country, Henley Court in Surrey. I motored down there this afternoon and caught sight of her in a market town close to the estate. She was with a group of young people, obviously on an afternoon out to visit the local pub and tour the village while visiting the country house."

Minerva sat down quite suddenly. The roll of paper slipped from her fingers. "Oh, thank goodness. And Mr. Culpepper?"

"I don't have any definitive news on him yet, but I was able to confirm that his office did send him to Edinburgh to meet with a client. It was a last-minute thing, according to Duck, Dade, and Croft. Apparently he makes the trip frequently. The firm has a difficult client in Edinburgh."

"How *did* you find out these details?"

"Trade secret."

Minerva gave me a brief smile, but then her face fell. "We're still in the same situation with Mr. Culpepper as we were with Diana. We haven't actually seen him."

"That's why I'm going to Edinburgh tomorrow."

"Oh, you can't do that. That's too much to ask—"

"It's no trouble. I don't have anything keeping me here. Traveling to Scotland will be the quickest way to find out if Mr. Culpepper really is in Edinburgh. Duck, Dade, and

Croft said Mr. Culpepper isn't due back in London for several days, and he's staying with his brother, who isn't on the telephone. Going there will be the most expedient thing to do."

"Oh. Well, someone has to go, but it should be me," she said as she glanced toward her desk. The sketches I'd looked at before the dinner party were still there, one still only partially inked and the other at the pencil stage. "I'm having difficulty concentrating. I can't seem to buckle down and get them finished." Her head dipped as she massaged her eyebrows. "And I haven't even thought about next week's edition. I have nothing. No thoughts. No ideas. Just a big blank."

"Which is completely understandable. Do you have any ideas that you had in the past but didn't have time to work on? Perhaps a list of possibilities?"

Minerva's head inched up. "Not a list, no." She spoke in a slow cadence as she eyed the sideboard. "I do have a file of sketches tucked away in a drawer that I abandoned for one reason or another."

"There you go. Perhaps you can find something in there?"

"I suppose I could." She shifted forward on the cushion as if she'd jump up and go look right at that moment. "Yes, I'm sure I can salvage something and rework it."

"Brilliant. So I'll go to Edinburgh tomorrow, and you'll stay here and finish the work you need to do. I have no other commissions. It's no trouble at all. And Jasper's there. I'll send him a telegram tonight and let him know I'm on my way."

"Oh." Minerva gave me a knowing look. "I'd forgotten Jasper was in Edinburgh. I don't feel guilty at all now."

"And you shouldn't. It's my job. Stop looking at me like that. I'm going to Edinburgh to check on Mr. Culpepper. Jasper being there happens to be coincidental."

"But a nice side benefit, nonetheless."

To avoid her teasing glance, I picked up the roll of paper Minerva had dropped on the floor. "What's this?" It was thick. Several long sheets had been rolled together.

"Blueprints." Minerva took it from me and spread it on the coffee table, unspooling the paper. She anchored one corner with her sketchbook and used a bowl of potpourri to hold the other.

I recognized the layout. "This is the second floor."

"It is. I told Evans that I was considering knocking down the wall between the living room and the sitting room, and that the architect I was working with was curious to know if there were any blueprints available."

"Evans had these?"

"He said he'd seen several rolls of paper on top of a cupboard in the office and that he'd check. He brought these up a couple of hours later, and I've been studying them ever since."

"What were you looking for?"

Minerva hunched over the drawing. "If I'm not mad and really did see a dead body in the hallway, it must've been put somewhere. Where did it go? We checked the attic and basement that first day, so it wasn't put in either of those places. Is it still here in South Regent Mansions? I don't think it is. By now, I think there would be . . ." She wrinkled her long nose. "An odor."

"Yes, I imagine so."

She tapped the square for the Kemps' old flat. "But to make absolutely sure, I had a look around the empty flat today. It seemed to be the most logical place to leave a dead body, if one were to discard such a thing here in the building. I asked Evans to open the flat for me."

"My, you've kept him busy."

"I have. After I had a look at the blueprints, I told him it would be so much easier to move to a new flat rather than knock down walls in here. There was absolutely nothing in 223." She swept her hand through the air as if she were dusting off a tabletop. "I poked my nose in every nook and cranny." She sat back against the sofa arm. "If the body isn't in the Kemps' old flat, what happened to it? Since no one has complained of an—um—odor, then there had to be some way to get it out of the building."

"The movers?"

Minerva shook her head. "Evans said they finished around half-past eleven, remember? With the lift out of order, the movers had to use the stairs. With the painters working their way down from the top floor, the movers wanted to get everything out as fast as possible so they wouldn't have to navigate around the painters."

"And you definitely left around a quarter to one?"

"Twelve forty-four. I'm completely sure of the time. I was running late and checked the clock as I left."

"So the movers were gone when you saw the rug."

"Yes. And if the painters *had* carted out a rolled rug, that would certainly have drawn Evans' notice."

"It would be the same situation with the lift repairman."

"Right." Minerva picked up her sketchbook, and the blueprints sprang back to their curved shape, rolling across the table to bump against the pot of potpourri that still pinned one side down. "I made a note of all the details I got from Evans."

She handed me the sketchbook. "My, he does keep exact notes, which helps us a great deal."

"I asked him if anyone moved any household belongings that day. Evans is adamant that no one brought anything like that down that day, and there were no visitors to South Regent Mansions Monday morning." She gave a little start as she said, "Oh, and when Evans opened the Kemps' old flat for me, I asked about the Darkwaith flat again. I made it seem as if I'd be interested in moving to that flat if it should become available. But no matter how I phrased it or hinted about it, he wouldn't give me one iota of information."

I looked away from her to the ceiling. "That is rather odd for Evans. He isn't one for idle chitchat, but he's never completely silent when it comes to the residents. If nothing else, his face is very expressive—especially if Mrs. Attenborough is mentioned. Once I asked him if Mrs. Attenborough was in—she dropped her scarf in the lift—and his widened eyes told me that I'd be better off waiting a few hours before knocking on her door."

"Yes, that's true," Minerva agreed, "but his face went rather strange went I mentioned flat 228. It was . . . hmm, how can I describe it? Carefully blank. Yes, that's it. It was as if he was working hard to not give anything away. I even told him I'd pay him for the information, but he shut down even more when I mentioned money."

I put the sketchbook down on the sofa as she unrolled the blueprints again. "Since I couldn't get anything out of Evans, I've concentrated on these." She smoothed the paper and anchored it with her hands. "I thought that perhaps there was some other way downstairs that I didn't know about or some connection between two of the flats, but I don't see anything of the kind."

She flipped through the blueprints. Each page represented a different floor. I peered over her shoulder as she shifted the oversized sheets. When she came to the last one, I said, "I agree. The only way to move between the flats on this floor and the other floors is by using either the lift or the back stairs."

Minerva removed her hands, and the pages popped back into a tube shape.

I shifted on the sofa cushion, and the sketchbook slid to the floor, landing facedown. "Oh, sorry."

"No worries. It's only drafts and notes." She picked it up and smoothed a wrinkled page.

One of the drawings on the page caught my eye. "Wait. May I?"

"Of course. I was sketching. I tend to do that whenever I'm out of sorts. Everyone here on the second floor is on my mind."

"Yes, I can see that." The page was covered with Minerva's sketches of each occupant of the second floor. The drawings were simple yet revealed something of the subject's personality. Minerva's economical strokes captured Mrs. Attenborough's patrician nose and haughty air. Diana, her chin tucked into a fur collar, looked up coquettishly from under the small brim of her cloche. Mr. Culpepper's trilby covered his sloping forehead and slightly receding hairline, and he was reaching to push his glasses up his nose, a habitual movement. Minerva had caught Mr. Culpepper's expression of mild standoffishness that was more a reserved detachment than an aloofness. "These are so good, Minerva. You caught them exactly. Not just their appearance, but their nature in only a few strokes. May I take this with me to Edinburgh?"

Minerva cocked her head. "Why?"

"Because it would be handy to have a picture to show the porters. I can see if any of them recognize Mr. Culpepper. He traveled First Class—or his office *says* he traveled First Class—and I intend to do the same."

Minerva gently tugged the page from the spine. "Excellent idea."

"I'm glad you sketched him with his trilby hat. I don't think I've ever seen him wear another."

Minerva said, "You know, now that you mention it, I haven't either. It's always the trilby with the little red feather."

"Which means he was probably wearing it when he went to Scotland." I stood up. "Now I must make sure I send a telegram off to Jasper. He planned to return to London tomorrow, but he might want to stay on for a few days since I'm traveling there."

"Oh, I'm sure he'll be delighted to rearrange his plans once he hears you're traveling to Scotland."

CHAPTER TEN

I closed my suitcase and clicked the latches into place. It was a new design, a lady's aeroplane case, which I had purchased after meeting a luggage salesman at a country home I visited over Christmas. While I wasn't planning a flight today, I certainly appreciated the fact that the suitcase was light and compact as I lifted it off my bed.

I surveyed my flat to make sure everything was in order, then picked up my handbag and the note I'd written for Constance. I had plenty of time to make it to King's Cross before the Flying Scotsman's departure time.

I stepped onto the crimson runner and locked the door to my flat. As I pocketed the key, the lift clinked to a stop. I bent and slid the note under the door of the flat next to mine, then darted to the lift so I wouldn't have to wait for it. But then I saw it was Constance on the other side of the gate, struggling with two string shopping bags, her handbag, and a large package. Even though her head was bent and I couldn't see her face, I knew at a glance that it was Constance, not Lola. I could tell from her darker blonde hair and from her stance with her feet planted firmly apart.

I pulled the gate open. "Here, let me help."

Constance looked up from the tangle of the shopping bag handles, twitching her head an inch to maneuver her long fringe out of her eyes. "Thank you."

"I just slipped a note under the door for you and Lola," I said. "I'm leaving London for a day or two, so I won't be able to speak with Lola when she returns today."

"Oh." Constance paused, her gaze darting down the hall, then back to me. "That's fine. In fact, Lola's decided to stay on for an indefinite time. She rang up this morning." Constance had tamed the handles of the shopping bags and transferred them to one hand along with her handbag. She tucked the package under her arm. "Sick relative, such a sad situation."

"I'm sorry to hear that. Where did you say Lola is?"

Constance opened her handbag and searched for her key. "Edinburgh."

"Well, that works out nicely. I must get her address from you." I checked my wristwatch. "I have time right now, if you don't mind. I have some paperwork I need to give to Lola. I'm on my way there today. I can take it to her directly instead of waiting for her to return. I'll just pop into my flat and get it ..."

Constance's brows sank below her fringe as she frowned. "That's not possible. I don't know exactly where she is in Edinburgh."

"Couldn't you ring her back and find out?"

"I don't have the number." Constance finally found her key and moved in the direction of the flat. "The connection was terrible, and we were cut off. Lola only intended to be gone a short time. Silly of her to not leave the address with me before she left, but that's Lola for you. Scatterbrained."

I walked with Constance down the hall. "But surely you know the family name? I wouldn't mind telephoning—"

"I'm not familiar with her relatives." Constance's tone, which had been friendly when I opened the lift's gate, had cooled a few degrees, conveying *I'm not your social secretary, so please sort this out among yourselves.* She inserted her key into the door lock.

I stepped back. "Of course. Sorry to be a bother. It's only that Lola was rather concerned about the information I have for her. I'd like to get it to her."

"Information?" Constance pivoted from the door so that she faced me. "What information?"

"It was nothing. Just a small favor." I wouldn't divulge anything else to Constance, even though she was Lola's roommate. I'd already let too much slip out.

Constance turned the lock and pushed the door open. "I suppose I'll eventually need a forwarding address since Lola doesn't know how long she'll be gone. I'll see what I can do for you."

"Thank you."

Constance nodded.

I drew a breath to tell her I'd be at the Premiere Hotel in Edinburgh, but she went into her flat before I could get the words out.

"I'll just ring you, then," I said to the closed door before I stepped into the lift, closed the gate, and punched the button for the ground floor.

My light suitcase meant I didn't need a porter, but as soon as I entered King's Cross, I handed the case off to the first porter who approached. As we threaded our way between other passengers and great trolleys of luggage, I held out the page with Minerva's drawing and pointed to her sketch of Mr. Culpepper. "Have you seen this man? It would have been a few days ago, on Monday."

We'd been striding along quickly, but now the porter halted and pushed back his hat to rub his hairline as he peered at the drawing. "No, miss."

"Are you sure? He would have been traveling alone without luggage. His trilby has a small red feather."

"I see hundreds of travelers every day. I can't remember all their faces."

"Of course not." We resumed walking.

Speaking to the porter was a long shot—especially since Mr. Culpepper had traveled without luggage. He wouldn't have needed a porter, but it seemed a shame to waste an opportunity to speak to someone who spent his entire day inside the train station. I'd hoped that Mr. Culpepper might have stood out because of his lack of luggage. Perhaps I'd have better luck on the train itself.

Further down the platform, the Flying Scotsman let out a blast of steam that engulfed the people standing near the engine. "Best hurry, miss," the porter said with a glance at the Roman numerals on the four-sided clock overhead, which showed one minute before ten o'clock. Both the porter and I picked up our pace as we headed for the teak carriages. I'd hoped to speak to a few more porters, but my encounter with Constance had me running late.

A whistle cut through the air as I turned sideways in the narrow corridor of the First Class carriage so that I could edge by other passengers on their way to different areas of the train.

The porter stowed my suitcase in the rack over my seat, doffed his cap after I tipped him, and sprinted for the door. "That was cutting it rather fine," I said.

Only one other seat of four in the area was occupied. A man sat next to the corridor, reading *The Times*. He inched the paper down, revealing only his nearly bald head, his high forehead, and a monocle on a gold chain. "Quite." Somehow he managed to convey censure with the single word. He rattled the newspaper as he raised it back so that it covered his face.

It appeared there would be no chitchat on this journey. My seat was diagonally across from the man by the window. I'd barely settled into it before the train gave a gentle lurch and began its slow roll out of the station. I put down the armrest between my seat and the empty one beside me. I placed Minerva's sketches on the armrest, then took my small notebook out of my handbag as the train climbed the steep ascent out of King's Cross.

While Minerva made sketches to sort out what was running through her mind, I made lists. I needed to get all the details I'd discovered in the last two days on paper. As

London slipped away, I applied myself to the task, jotting down everything I'd learned about the inhabitants of the second floor of South Regent Mansions. The light flickered as we moved in and out of two tunnels, then the track leveled out, and the train flew across Bedfordshire with its farmland spreading out in a wide vista. The day was bright, and sun picked out the furrows in the soil, highlighting one side and throwing the other into shadow.

The conductor arrived and came to me first. The man with the newspaper had folded the paper and taken out a book, but he'd fallen asleep, his chin resting on his chest. His monocle dangled from the chain, swaying with the motion of the train. The book rested in his lap, his hands loose on the edges of the covers.

I handed my ticket to the conductor, then swiveled Minerva's drawings so that they faced him. "One moment, please. Do you remember seeing this man on the train?" I pointed to Mr. Culpepper.

His gaze flickered across the page. "No, miss." He turned and touched the man's shoulder to wake him. I squashed a sigh and went back to my notes. I skimmed what I'd written down and decided I needed something more streamlined, like a chart of some sort. No, a timetable—that was exactly what would help me keep everyone's movements straight. I paged back and forth through my notes, then sat back to study the results:

11:30 - Movers finish
12:00 - Painters leave for lunch

12:30 - I leave my flat and see the rug on my way to the stairs
12:35 - Lift repairman finishes
12:44 - Minerva leaves, takes lift, and sees carpet
12:48 (approximate) - Minerva goes back up in the lift and the carpet is gone

Looking at it written down so neatly made me realize that whoever removed the rug after Minerva saw it couldn't have taken it far. Even with the lift stopping on the first floor before reaching the lobby and traveling back up to the second floor, it couldn't have taken more than four or five minutes. Someone had dragged that rug into one of the flats on the second floor. I was sure of it.

Unfortunately, I couldn't draw any other conclusions. Anyone on the second floor could have nipped out and dragged the rug into their flat. Or, if someone kept a copy of a latchkey for a neighbor, they might even use another flat to "store" the rug until they could move the body. The Kemps' empty flat would be a perfect temporary storage location. But no matter where they stashed the body, how in the world did the murderer get the body *out* of South Regent Mansions? Evans said no one had moved any household goods out Monday afternoon, and it hadn't been in the attic or the basement.

The man across from me began to snore. At first, the noise was only a minor annoyance, but as his snuffling became louder, I finally gave up and put my notebook away. I couldn't concentrate. I took out a novel I'd brought along, a crime story, the second one to feature a funny little French detective, Inspector Hanaud. I'd just settled back against the cushiony seat when we came to a canal. It cut across the farmland on a diagonal. The railway skimmed over the wide swath of water dotted with barges. Once we were beyond it, I opened my book and immersed myself in the puzzle of *The House of the Arrow*.

I was several chapters into the story when the sleeping man's snores reached a crescendo. He awoke with a start and peered out the window. "Goodness, we're nearly at York."

I looked up from the pages of my book. "I'm sorry?" I was so wrapped up in the story that it took me a second to return from the fictional setting of France to the present reality of the interior of the carriage.

He motioned to the window. "There's Abbey Church. See the three towers? We'll be in York shortly. The dining car will be overrun soon." He tucked his book into his bag and departed.

I checked my watch and was surprised to see that the journey was nearly half over. I finished the chapter I was reading, then made my way to the dining car as another train rattled by us on the next track, speeding toward London.

I met two of the train's attendants on the way and asked each one if they recognized the sketch of Mr. Culpepper, but neither showed the least spark of recognition. Contrary to my traveling companion's prediction, there were plenty of seats in the dining car.

I had a table to myself and enjoyed an excellent meal of

potage Albion, cod in parsley sauce, York ham, salad, and vegetables with sultana pudding, followed by cheese and biscuits. As I finished my coffee, I studied the view. Thick woods dominated the landscape with flashes of icy rivers showing among the trees. The waiter, who was gray-haired and a bit tottery, cleared away my empty coffee cup. "Will there be anything else, miss?"

"Only a quick question." I took Minerva's sketches from my handbag and pointed to Mr. Culpepper. "Do you remember this man? I believe he took this train on Monday."

The waiter's glance as he looked up from the paper back to me was pitying. "No, I'm afraid I don't." He hesitated, then said, "It's none of my business, miss, but sometimes young men do not want to be found. You're a nice young lady. I'm sure he's not worth your trouble."

"Oh, it's nothing like that. I'm helping a friend."

"Ah." His tone said he didn't believe me. "Well, in any case, I'm afraid I don't remember him. But this woman"—he touched the sketch of Lola—"she was here in the dining car" —the wrinkles in his forehead deepened—"on Monday? Yes, I believe it was Monday. Eggs, dry toast, and black coffee."

"Really?" I asked.

"Oh yes, I'm sure. It's the hat, you see. Hers was green, like crème de menthe." He pointed to the sketch of Lola. "It matched the woman's coat. Striking, she was."

Minerva hadn't added any color to the sketches. They were simply pencil drawings, but Minerva had drawn Lola wearing the mint-green cloche with the little feather. When

Lola paired the hat with her favorite coat, which was a matching color, she was memorable.

"Thank you. You've been very helpful." I pushed back the chair from the linen-covered table. I took a few steps, then turned back. "Did she have a companion? Perhaps this man?" I pointed to Mr. Culpepper's face.

"No, she dined alone."

CHAPTER ELEVEN

The rest of the journey to Edinburgh passed uneventfully. When I returned from the dining car, my traveling companion was using his briefcase as a makeshift desk. He'd spread his stack of papers across it and tucked his monocle between his cheekbone and eyebrow. He glanced up when I arrived, gave me a brief nod of greeting, then returned to his notations.

I settled into my seat and picked up my book, but I couldn't concentrate on the story. I finally put it away as we approached Durham with its cathedral and castle rising on the hillside above the city. I enjoyed the view but in a disassociated way. My thoughts were too busy running through possible implications of the news that Lola had traveled on the Flying Scotsman on Monday.

There was a slight possibility that the waiter was mistaken, but he'd described the color of Lola's hat and coat exactly. In my experience, men were not incredibly observant about fashion—with Jasper being the exception. He was a bit of a clotheshorse, so he was always aware of the attire, but most men seemed like my father and my uncle, who couldn't tell you five minutes after they'd spoken to a woman if her dress had been purple or red. But Lola's mint-green coat and hat were striking, and the waiter had said his wife had a hat in that exact shade.

Had Lola and Mr. Culpepper traveled to Scotland together? I'd never seen any interaction between the two of them—not even during Minerva's dinner party when they'd both been in attendance. Was there a reason that they wouldn't dine at the same table if they were traveling together? Unless, perhaps, there was something nefarious going on?

We skimmed along the rails, the train scooping up water from the troughs as we made our way north. As we passed more castles and crossed the border into Scotland, I turned my thoughts to Mr. Culpepper's brother and considered how I should approach him. With any luck, I'd find him home this evening—and Mr. Culpepper with him. What reason could I use for my visit? It was quite a journey to travel from London to Scotland to merely speak to someone.

I decided on the truth, albeit a shortened version of it. I was working for a client who wanted me to locate each person who lived on the second floor of South Regent Mansions. If questions followed that simple explanation, I'd say I wasn't allowed to share anything else, and I'd imply that I was as in the dark as well.

The cadence of the train shifted as it climbed the incline of the wooded hills, which were dusted with a layer of snow. As we neared Edinburgh, I caught sight of the silver flash, which was the Firth of Forth. Then we reached the outskirts of the city, and buildings rose up and cut off the view, except a couple of quick glimpses of Arthur's Seat as the train slowed. It ran through a short tunnel, then into Waverly Station.

Jasper was waiting for me on the platform, and a little burst of happiness bloomed in my chest when I saw him looking dapper but rather bored as he twirled the chain of his monocle. While Jasper's eyes were weak and he required glasses for reading, the monocle, like his ebony walking stick, was more the mark of a fashionable gentleman than an aid for reading. He had a perfectly ordinary set of spectacles with a powerful prescription that he carried tucked away in his pocket for close work. I waved, and Jasper's pose of ennui dropped away as a smile spread across his face. I threaded through the press of the crowd.

"Hello, old bean," he said. "It really is you."

"Of course it's me." I tilted my cheek up for him to kiss, and enjoyed the brief warmth of his lips on my skin. "Why do you look surprised? I told you I'd arrive today."

"After I changed my train ticket, I suddenly thought someone might be having me on."

"You thought I might have sent the telegram as a rag? I'd never joke about traveling across England." The telegram I'd sent him read, *Arrive Edinburgh tomorrow - stop - On a case.*

I'd received his reply before I left that morning. *Game is afoot - stop - Your Watson awaits.*

Jasper reached for my suitcase. "But some of my friends

would. They'd think it was great fun if I fell for something like that."

"Well, this is no joke. I'm working."

"So I gathered. How was the journey?"

"I discovered something unexpected." I hooked my arm through his as we set off across the platform. After the close air of the carriage, the brisk air felt wonderful.

"Of course you did. You always do. I stand ready to perform any Watson-like duties. My calendar is clear for you."

I stopped walking. "Jasper, I didn't mean you needed to drop everything and wait for me. I'm perfectly capable of handling things if you need to return to London. I sent the telegram because I thought you'd want to know I was on my way to Edinburgh."

"Exactly right. I have no pressing engagements in London—well, except for my tailor. He's happy to reschedule." Jasper took a step forward to the exit, but I didn't move.

"Are you here . . . officially?"

"You forget, darling, that I'm never *anywhere* officially."

I grinned at his quip. "Are you here unofficially, then?"

"No. I attended the book auction for my own pleasure. And now you're here, which makes the trip doubly pleasurable."

I felt my cheeks heat up under his gaze, and I was grateful for the gust of frigid wind that swept across the platform. I was suddenly too warm all over. "Well, you may not feel that way after I drag you across Edinburgh. I intend to get right to work."

"I expected nothing less." He extended his arm. "Although, I'm a little in the dark."

"I'll fill you in on the way to the hotel. I'm staying at the Premier."

Jasper signaled for a taxi. "Excellent. I'm there as well."

By the time we'd dropped off my suitcase at the hotel and were in another taxi on the way to the address of Mr. Culpepper's brother, I'd given Jasper the details on why I was in Edinburgh. He was discreet, and I knew he'd never share what I told him. Society might think he was a bit of a rattle—a view he intentionally cultivated with his monocle and droll manners—but I knew that he had more depth and seriousness than people gave him credit for.

The hotel was situated on the Royal Mile with a view of Edinburgh Castle.

"Have you seen the castle?" Jasper asked as the taxi drove away from the hotel.

"Once. Father brought me here when I was a child. I only remember it being extremely cold."

"Then perhaps we can visit it this evening."

"Perhaps." I wasn't on a tour.

"Yes, to work," Jasper said, turning to look out the front of the taxi, which was moving away from the center of the city. "And you think Minerva really saw"—he glanced at the back of the driver's head and lowered his voice—"a foot?"

"Minerva's one of the most levelheaded people I know. I don't think she had a—oh, I don't know—a hallucination or something along those lines."

"No, Minerva wouldn't. But that means she should speak to the—er—officials."

"She can't. Her boss at the newspaper would fire her if there was any whiff of trouble. And she's sure the officials will hone in on her."

"Well, if she were to come forward now, they certainly would. It would look fishy to them."

"Quite."

Mr. Culpepper's brother lived in Colinton, which was a hilly area, dense with trees. The streets were lined with stone walls and high hedges. I couldn't really see much of the houses behind their screening shrubbery.

The driver navigated up one of the hills, then pulled to the side of the road. "Here you are." He rolled to a stop next to a tiny flat-front house of slate and stone with small-paned windows on either side of a pea-green door. As the taxi driver pulled away, Jasper and I looked up and down the road, which was lined with more small houses, some of them stone and others covered in harling. "It's like a row of dollhouses," I said as we went through a hip-high gate, then crossed the front garden in three steps.

"What's our reason for trekking all the way from London to appear on this man's doorstep with questions about his brother?"

I knocked briskly. "I'm on a case. Isn't that reason enough?" A few moments later, a man swung the door open. The resemblance between him and Mr. Culpepper was striking. While Mr. Culpepper was lanky and lean and this man was shorter and stout, they both had a similar facial structure of a sloping forehead that rose from flat eyebrows to a hairline that was beginning to recede at the temples.

His eyes were also the same shade of pale blue as Mr. Culpepper's.

If their facial similarities hadn't assured me that this was a relative of Mr. Culpepper's, the fact that the man used his index finger to push his spectacles up the bridge of his nose as he swung open the door clinched the matter. It so exactly matched Mr. Culpepper's mannerism that if this man hadn't been a different height and weight, I could have mistaken him for Mr. Culpepper.

He looked at Jasper, but I stepped up and said, "Hello, I'm Olive Belgrave, and I'm looking for a Mr. Culpepper, who normally resides in London. His office told me I could find him here."

"I'm sorry, but you're a little late." A trace of a Scottish burr rolled through his words.

"Late? Isn't he here?"

"No, he finished his business this morning and departed for London."

I let out a sigh. He'd been on one of those trains whizzing by me today, and I hadn't even known it.

"Was it something urgent? And why are you looking for my brother? Is something wrong?"

"No, nothing's wrong." I pushed away my frustration at missing Mr. Culpepper. "I'm conducting a private inquiry and need to clear up a few details." I took out my notebook and pencil. "Your brother arrived when?"

"Private inquiry? Who are you?"

"I'm afraid that information is confidential."

The man reached to close the door, but Jasper leaned in.

"We're doing a survey for the Society of Citizen Knowledge. SOCK."

The man paused, and I chimed in, abandoning my original plan of attack, which wasn't working. "On travel statistics. We only have two or three questions, if we might have another moment of your time. We need to complete the data on your brother. We have down that he left London on Monday morning and arrived here that evening. Is that correct?"

"Well, yes."

"Excellent." I made a check mark in my notebook. "What were his thoughts on the journey from London?" I asked, pencil poised.

"Fine, I suppose. He didn't say much about it." He stepped back and closed the door a few inches.

"And his companion?" I said quickly. "What was her opinion?" I used my most businesslike tone.

That caught his attention and arrested his movement to close the door. "He didn't have a companion. He traveled alone."

"Are you sure? I have a reference that he traveled with a woman named—let's see—Lola."

He shook his head. "No, that's not right. You'd better double-check your information. He's never mentioned a Lola."

"Thank you so much" —the door closed and the lock clicked— "for your time," I said as I turned away. "Well, that didn't go quite as I'd hoped."

"Not bad overall." Jasper held the gate for me. "I'm

feeling peckish. I see a pub down the road. Fancy a shepherd's pie?"

"Sounds wonderful." We set off down the street toward the little village, making for the swinging pub sign. Over our meal, I said, "So much for my idea of tossing around the term *inquiry agent* and getting answers. Your scheme worked much better."

"I find that the acronym helps. People are trying to work out in their head what the letters stand for, and it's easier to slip a question in and get an answer while they're matching up the letters with the words in their mind."

"It certainly worked just now."

"It was Mr. Culpepper's brother, then?" Jasper asked. "And do you think he was telling the truth?"

"Yes, on both counts. There's a definite family resemblance. And I do think he was telling the truth. He didn't seem to be making up responses or assessing how we took his replies. He wasn't concerned at all about whether or not we believed him."

"He did act as if he'd never heard the name Lola."

"Which puts a rather large hole in my theory about Lola and Mr. Culpepper traveling together. But she is here in Edinburgh . . . somewhere. I'll telephone Constance from the hotel and see if she's obtained Lola's address."

Jasper set down his empty pint and consulted his wristwatch. "I believe we could work in a quick tour around the castle before we return to the hotel."

"Sounds lovely."

The castle itself was closed, but we climbed the hill and saw the massive stone walls as well as the portcullis gate. It was as cold as I remembered from my childhood visit. By the time we meandered back down the hill and strolled along the Royal Mile to the hotel, I was chilled to the bone. Jasper went to the bar to get us a table by the fire while I went through the lobby to the telephone kiosk.

CHAPTER TWELVE

"*A*ny luck?" Jasper asked as I joined him in the hotel bar.

Sparks flitted up from the tall orange and red flames of the fire. I felt warmer just looking at it. I settled into the club chair and enjoyed the heat of the blaze as it wrapped around me. "No answer. Constance must be out. The operator let it ring and ring. And I was so hoping that Constance would have found out where Lola's family lives. Edinburgh is too large to visit each of the Mallorys listed in the directory."

"Mallorys?" Jasper asked.

"Lola's full name is Delores Mallory."

"I see."

A waiter arrived with a tray of drinks, and Jasper said, "I ordered hot toddies."

"Topping idea." I wrapped my hands around the warm cup. "The front desk had a directory, and I checked to see how many Mallorys are listed here in Edinburgh. Two pages."

"That *is* rather a lot."

"Yes. It doesn't make sense for me to contact each one. I don't even know if Lola is visiting relatives on her mother's side or her father's side. If it's her mother's family, the surname will be completely different." After speaking to Constance in the hallway, I'd returned to my flat to retrieve Lola's report so I'd have it with me in Edinburgh in case I was able to track her down.

I sipped the hot toddy and enjoyed the sensation of it warming me from the inside. "It's such a shame not to be able to hand off my report to her now that I'm in the same city as she is. Not to mention that I'd like to speak to her about traveling up on the Flying Scotsman on the same day as Mr. Culpepper. Although, it does look as if it was a coincidence that they were both on the same train."

Jasper smoothed down his cuffs. "That's possible. The Flying Scotsman is the train to take if one is traveling from London to Edinburgh. They might both have been on the same train on the same day and not realized it."

The desk clerk approached our table. "Miss Belgrave, telegram for you."

A flutter of anxiety skittered through me. I thanked him and took the envelope as I exchanged a look with Jasper. Father and Sonia were still in Italy. The last letter I'd had from Sonia said Father's health was improving and that his cough had all but disappeared, but one never knew ...

I tore it open, and my worry melted away. "It's from Minerva. She says Mr. Culpepper *has* returned to London, and she's spoken to him." I put the telegram in my pocket with a sigh and picked up my hot toddy. "If I'd simply waited one more day, Minerva and I would have had our answer about Mr. Culpepper." I looked at Jasper over the rim of the cup. "But I'm not sorry to have made the trip, though."

"I'm delighted you made the journey north." The skin around his eyes crinkled as he smiled. "Even if it was for a case. Then you plan to return to London tomorrow?"

"As much as I'm enjoying spending time with you here in Edinburgh, yes, I should go back to London. Now that we know Mr. Culpepper is fine, that only leaves flat 228."

"Ah, the mysterious Darkwaiths."

"Yes, and I have no idea how to go about checking on them."

"Are the inhabitants of the flat always referred to in the plural?"

I set down my cup slowly as I searched my memory. "I'd never thought about it, but yes, they are."

"Interesting."

"I'll definitely need to sort how many people actually live in the flat," I said.

"If anyone knows, it will be the porter or the maids."

"Minerva's already spoken to the porter. If Evans knows anything, he's not giving it away. Although, Minerva said he had an odd reaction when she asked about the Darkwaiths. She said his face went completely blank, which isn't like him. He's not reticent. And I've asked the maids about the Darkwaiths before. They don't use the building's maid service. They have their own help in."

"I'm sure we can think of something. After all, we'll have eight hours on the train tomorrow to brainstorm. And if we can't come up with something then, I can hand off the theater tickets, and we'll keep at it."

"Oh, that's right! *The End of the Line!*" Jasper had tickets for the most popular play in London. He'd asked me weeks ago if I'd like to accompany him. "With all that's going on at South Regent Mansions, it slipped my mind, but there's no reason to give the tickets away. After all, I can only do so much where the Darkwaiths are concerned. We're to the point that Minerva may have to contact the police if we can't make headway with discovering who actually lives in flat 228."

"You'll contact Longly?"

"Yes, I think that would be best. He'll frown and fuss about the wait, but he will listen to Minerva. He won't dismiss her story or think she's barmy. The difficulty will be convincing Minerva to speak to him. She won't like going to him without knowing exactly what the situation is with flat 228. I'll have to think of something."

"You may have to break in, old bean."

"Welcome home, Miss Belgrave. Good evening, Mr. Rimington," Evans said as Jasper and I entered South Regent Mansions the next afternoon.

"Thank you, Evans," I said. "Any messages for me?"

"No, Miss Belgrave."

"Really? Nothing? I was expecting a message from the Darkwaiths."

A flash of something—was it amusement?—flicked across Evans' face, but it was gone before I could identify it. He turned away to double-check the cubbyholes behind his counter. "No, nothing." His face was as empty as a chalkboard that had been wiped clean. Evans picked up his pen and bent over his ledger. "I hope you have a pleasant evening, Miss Belgrave." His tone was a dismissal.

Jasper and I exchanged a glance. We'd had a long talk on the train about how to get information out of Evans. Jasper was all for offering cash, but when I told him Minerva had already attempted it and been rebuffed, we came up with other plans of attack—my little subterfuge about the message was the first tactic. I'd hoped to catch Evans off guard and that he'd slip up and release some information. But I could see I'd have to move on to my last plan of attack—the truth.

Jasper stepped forward, and I took my suitcase from him. "I'll return in a few hours, old bean," he said. "Shall we dine after the theater?"

As I leaned in to buss his cheek, I inhaled his citrusy scent. "Yes. Then we won't be rushed."

He flared an eyebrow, and I felt the blood rush into my cheeks as I blushed. That man and his looks! He could say so much with a glance. Or maybe I was just better at reading him now. He mouthed *good luck*, then, hands in his trouser pockets, strolled down the crimson runner. The doorman swung open the glass door for him.

I turned back to Evans, who was still writing in the

ledger. I addressed the top of his hat. "I admit that comment about the message from the Darkwaiths was a little ploy. I realize that whatever secret you've been charged with keeping, you're taking it seriously." Evans' head popped up, and I leaned forward. In a confiding tone, I said, "While we're all curious about the Darkwaiths, I'm not poking my nose in because of idle curiosity. Something's come up that—well—it's extremely important that I get in touch with whoever lives there. You know the residents, don't you?"

Evans brushed his hand over the page of his ledger, soothing down the paper. "That's private information."

Before he looked down again, I said quickly, "You know my line of work, Evans."

"Snooping, isn't it?"

Inwardly I bristled, but he wasn't being snide. His face was open and his eyebrows were raised slightly as if he was waiting for me to confirm his guess as to my occupation.

"Private inquiry agent," I corrected. "I'm looking into something that happened here at South Regent Mansions." The ledger was forgotten. I now had Evans' complete attention. "If I can't find out who lives in that flat and speak to them, then I'm afraid I'll have to contact the police."

He blinked. "The police?"

"It's a very serious matter."

Evans stared at me a moment, then one corner of his mouth curved up. "Excellent try, Miss Belgrave."

He was entertained, I realized. He was laughing—at me.

He added, "I must keep my counsel. I'm sworn to secrecy." His tone changed from chiding to fatherly. "I'd advise against contacting the police. It will only be rather embar-

MURDER AT THE MANSIONS

rassing . . . for you." He picked up his pen and bent over his ledger.

Defeated, I turned to the lift, mentally marking Evans off my list. The lift reached the second floor, and I pulled the gate back. I'd have to find some other way to figure out who lived in flat 228.

"Olive!" Minerva hurried down the scarlet runner. "I'm so glad you're back."

"What's happened to you? You look as if you've been cleaning." Her skirt was crumpled, her cuffs were streaked with dust, and a black smear ran down her long nose and across a cheekbone.

"What?"

I pointed to my own nose and cheek. "You have a smudge."

She scrubbed her face. "Oh, that. It's probably from the attic. I've been searching the building for hours, and I've finally figured it out."

"Figured what out?"

"How they got the body out."

CHAPTER THIRTEEN

A few moments later, after I'd stowed my suitcase in my flat, I followed Minerva down the corridor, hurrying to keep up with her fast pace.

"I've been studying the blueprints of South Regent Mansions again," she said over her shoulder, "There's a closet at the end of the corridor on most of the floors."

"Is there? I've never noticed."

"On all the other floors, the space on the blueprints is simply a square that's labeled as storage. But on the ground floor, the first floor, and this floor, the blueprints have an X over that same area. So I had a look around. Beginning on the third floor, the area is simply a storage closet filled with cleaning supplies and a few odds and ends. But not here."

We'd reached the wall at the far end of the corridor. Flat 228, the Darkwaiths' flat, was on one side. Miss Attenborough's flat, 229, was across the hall from it. Next to her door was a short hallway that led to the back stairs.

Minerva swept a hand toward the wall in front of us. "Look. Do you see it?"

At first I didn't understand what she meant, but then I spotted the small white handle above the wainscoting. Painted the same color as the walls, it blended in. Now that I'd seen the handle, I could pick out the faint seam that ran from the skirting board to a point a foot or two above our heads, then ran parallel with the ceiling until it met another seam that ran down again to the skirting board.

I traced my finger along one of the seams. "It's a recessed door. It's easy to miss."

"Right. It's designed so that it doesn't stand out. I suppose the architects thought a great hulking door at the end of the hall would interrupt the lines, and this building is all about beautiful flowing lines."

"I suppose so," I said. "I'd never thought about it, but you're the artist, so you'd notice things like that."

"I wish I'd seen it before today because what's behind this door is vastly interesting." She turned the handle and pulled the door open, revealing a brick wall.

"A brick wall?" I looked from it to Minerva. "That's strange. It's not something you'd expect to see in a new building." If South Regent Mansions had been an older building that had been renovated, a bricked-off area wouldn't be that unusual, but the service flats were new.

"Right. And it's the same on the first floor—another brick wall. While Evans was busy with a delivery, I managed to take a peek on the ground floor in the lobby. It's exactly the same there too—a recessed door with a brick wall behind it."

"Why would someone brick up a closet? That doesn't make sense."

"Oh, but it does if this space"—she patted the brick wall —"is something other than a closet, like, say, a private lift." Minerva swung the door closed. "The same area in the basement is blocked off on the blueprints, but it doesn't have an X on it and it isn't labeled as storage."

"That's a big leap," I said. "It could be something completely different. Maybe something to do with the plumbing or heating."

"It's the only thing out of the ordinary about this building and"—Minerva's gaze shifted over my shoulder. She lowered her voice as she added—"the bricked-off area shares a wall with flat 228." Minerva was right; the north wall of the bricked-off area would be against the south wall of flat 228.

"Have you been down to the basement?" I asked.

"No. I was on my way there when you arrived."

"Then I'm going with you." I turned to go to the lift, but Minerva caught my arm.

She said, "We have to take the stairs. The lift doesn't go down to the basement."

"Oh, that's right. I'd forgotten." We went down the hallway to the back stairs. This staircase was rather plain and steep. No plush carpeting or wainscoting, only bare wooden stair treads and white walls. We went past the landings for the first floor, then the ground floor until we came to the door with the letter B painted on it. Minerva swung it open, and we stepped into the darkness. "There's got to be a light around here somewhere."

When we'd checked the basement earlier in the week, we'd brought torches and hadn't bothered to switch on the lights, but neither of us had thought to bring them along this time. I patted along the wall. "No switch here."

"Perhaps it's a chain." Minerva's voice floated out of the blackness " . . . ah, here we are."

There was a metallic jingle, then a single bulb suspended from the ceiling came on, illuminating a small circle of the basement. "Here's another, and then one after it." Minerva walked down the narrow space, then went up on her tiptoes to reach more of the dangling chains.

"Good thing you're tall," I said. "I'd never reach those without a stepladder."

"I'm sure there's one around here—not that we could find it," Minerva said as she came back to where I stood. The circles of light didn't extend far. The basement walls were in shadow. "I don't really want to know what's in the dark corners down here. Probably a rat or two." She grimaced. "Come on, let's make this quick."

"I'd rather not linger either. At least it shouldn't take long. The basement isn't as large as the entire building." When we'd checked the basement on Monday, we'd only been interested in looking for a rolled carpet. We hadn't examined the rest of the space in great detail.

"No, I could see that on the blueprints," Minerva said. "The builders didn't excavate the whole footprint of the building. The basement is only slightly wider than the corridor that runs the length of the building. There's just enough room for the rubbish lifts." Minerva waved a hand at the steel doors that lined both sides of the open walkway.

They were about two feet high, and each of the doors was labeled with a number.

"Oh, I see, the numbers correspond to the flat numbers above." I was standing beside a door labeled *28*. The metal door across from it was *29*.

"Right," Minerva said, but her voice was distracted as she paced back and forth in front of the wall near the back stairs, which was plastered, unlike the rest of the exposed brick walls. "Why didn't I bring a torch? The light from those bulbs is incredibly dim."

South Regent Mansions touted itself as having modern conveniences—up-to-date kitchens, maid service, an on-site kitchen, and rubbish lifts. I moved a few steps further into the basement. "I've never thought much about how the rubbish is removed." About halfway down the walkway, a ramp went up to a door with a small window at eye level. "That goes to the back courtyard?" I asked.

Minerva looked over her shoulder. "Yes, that must be how they remove the rubbish each day."

A couple of large carts were pushed back against the walls. I imagined the rubbish bins from the flats were emptied into the carts, which were then pushed up the ramp and emptied when the waste lorries arrived.

Minerva ran her hand over the plaster. "It should be around here."

I returned to her side. "Here, let me help. Are you looking for another recessed door?"

"Yes, but you might as well let me do it. I'm already dusty, and you'll get that gorgeous travel suit dirty if you pitch in."

"Maybe I can get you more light." I dragged a crate out of the shadows and lined it up under the nearest light. I climbed up, grabbed the wire that extended from the ceiling, and aimed the bulb toward the wall Minerva was inching along.

"Oh, thank you. That's much better. Here it is. It's exactly like the doors upstairs, with a small handle—except this one has a keyhole under it. Oh, I hope it's not—" She twisted and tugged, but the door didn't budge. "It *is* locked. How frustrating! I don't suppose your discreet detecting skills include the ability to pick a lock?"

"Unfortunately, no."

"Too bad Jasper isn't here," Minerva said. "He's a resourceful chap. I bet he'd know how."

"He doesn't know either."

One of Minerva's arched eyebrows inched higher. "Really? Very interesting that you know that about him. Remind me to ask you later how you came to have that knowledge."

I stepped down from the crate. "Believe me, I'm beginning to think it's a skill at least one of us might need to acquire."

Minerva and I stood side by side and regarded the recessed door. "It must go somewhere," she said. "Otherwise, why would it be locked?"

"It might be another storage closet."

"With a shiny lock on it? When none of the other storage closets were locked? No." She shook her head. "I'm sure it connects to the Darkwaiths' flat. It's the only thing that makes sense. Everyone else is accounted for. The body must have been someone from flat 228 and this"—Minerva hit her palm against the door—"is how the murderer got the body out."

"We'll just have to figure out another way to discover who lives in flat 228."

"How? Evans won't speak to us, and no one has ever seen the Darkwaiths. Short of picking this lock and seeing what's behind this door, I don't see how we can find out." Minerva's voice had crept louder and louder as she spoke. She blew out a breath. "I'm sorry, Olive. I didn't mean to shout at you. I thought I was so close to finding out what happened. I can't sleep for thinking about that awful pale foot sticking out of the carpet and wondering who was bundled up in there and carted away."

Now her voice wavered on the last few words. I knew she was close to tears, and that worried me. Minerva was a rock—steady and even tempered. The fact that she'd slammed her hand against the recessed door and now she was swallowing in that way one does when one is desperately fighting down emotion—well, she was clearly distraught.

"I know what we have to do. Jasper said it earlier. We have to break into the Darkwaiths' flat."

If Jasper had been here, he would have made light of my statement and probably would have said something about mountaineering being frowned on in central London, but Minerva took a steadying breath. "How? Climb down from the roof? That would be dangerous. There's nothing to hang on to, no ornate trim or fancy molding."

"No, nothing like that. We can go in from here." I

pointed to the rubbish lift marked *28*. "They're not locked." I pulled on the steel door. It slid back, revealing a dumb-waiter type platform. A ripe scent of old meat and sodden papers floated out. I ignored it and turned to the pair of heavy chains that ran up the wall. I tugged on one. A platform labeled with the number *1* inched lower, descending into view. A few more tugs, and another platform, this one labeled *2*, descended.

"How clever," I said. "As the platforms are lowered, they stack up. The rubbish bin is removed from each platform and then . . ." I grabbed the other chain and pulled. The platform reversed course and ascended, disappearing from view. "Pull down on this chain, and the platforms come down. Pull on the other, and they go up."

I went back to the other chain and lowered the platforms until the one labeled with a *2* appeared. A circular rubbish bin sat on the platform. "Perfect." I removed it. "I'll climb in here. You pull the chain down, which will raise the platform up to the second floor. Simple."

Minerva scanned the platform. "I don't know. It's awfully small."

"Which is why I'm going up. You'd never fit. I'll listen once you raise me up to the second floor. If it's quiet, I'll slip into the flat and have a look around." The door that concealed the rubbish lift in my flat was held closed with a magnetized latch. It wouldn't be hard to get out of the rubbish lift.

"But someone might be inside the flat," Minerva's tone was scandalized.

"I don't think so. The rubbish bin was still on the platform," I pointed out. "Do you leave your rubbish bin on the platform?"

"No . . ." Minerva said slowly. "But they might have forgotten."

"Minerva, it's late. If anyone was home in two twenty-eight, they would have had dinner by now. They'd have opened the door and taken out the bin so they could clear away their dinner." The bins were emptied each morning and returned, so the fact that the one for flat 228 sat on the platform this late in the day indicated that the flat was empty.

"Unless they dined out."

"That's possible, I suppose. I'll be careful. I'll tap on the platform, three quick raps, if I want you to lower me down." I demonstrated, and the tinny sound rang out.

"All right, but only five minutes, and then I'm bringing it back down. That will be all my nerves can stand."

"Fine." I glanced at my watch. "Five minutes from when I get to the second floor." I took a deep breath, then ducked into the opening.

CHAPTER FOURTEEN

I folded myself into the minuscule space of the rubbish lift. I drew my legs up to my chest and wrapped my skirt around them. With my chin tucked, I just barely fit.

Minerva pulled on the chain, and the platform rose in jerky increments. An initial clatter of metal announced my departure from the basement, but after that first jangle of noise, the platform rose in silence. Within a few seconds, the dim light thrown out by the bare bulbs in the basement faded, and there was only inky black. I was passing the ground floor where there was no access to the rubbish lift.

I hadn't thought I was afraid of small, closed-in places— I'd played Sardines with my cousins when we were young— but there was a definite difference in those childhood games and being shut into a tiny area with no exit.

I found it extremely unpleasant. The confined area seemed to magnify the heavy odors of food that had gone off. The bumpy stop-and-go movement only increased my dislike of the situation. I was suddenly very aware of the enclosing metal walls that pressed against my back and shoulders. I lifted my head a fraction, and it connected immediately with the ceiling of the platform. I scrunched down like a turtle retreating into its shell. What if the chain broke, or what if something happened to Minerva? If she stopped pulling the platform up, I'd be trapped in the rubbish lift in total darkness.

I pushed those horrible thoughts away, and I tried to ignore my increasing heart rate. I wiped my sweaty palms on my skirt and refolded it more precisely around my ankles. I forced myself to picture the platform climbing upward away from the enclosing walls of the ground floor.

The platform inched higher, and a drop of pale yellow turned into a long thread of light that seeped through the seam around the cupboard door that closed off the rubbish lift. I'd reached the first floor. A snatch of conversation and a few notes of the wireless program filtered through the cupboard door, and I breathed easier.

Minerva must have gotten into a rhythm because I was rising faster. The blackness snuffed out the seam of light as I rose, then the platform stopped moving. I was on the second floor now.

I traced my fingers around the wall where the seam of light had showed the cupboard door on the lower floor. The varnish that covered the cupboard doors was smooth under my fingertips. No light came in around the edge of this cupboard door, which was a good sign.

My fingers connected with the cool metal of the

magnetic catch. I pushed on it gently, causing a faint click as the latch disengaged. I opened it the merest sliver.

No light. No sound. I waited a few more seconds, then pushed it wide and extracted myself from the diminutive space, breathing in air that didn't smell of aging vegetables. I rotated my shoulders and shook out my arms as I scanned what I could see of the kitchen in the darkness. The counters were clear, and the empty sink glowed a ghostly white in the dimness.

I moved on my tiptoes across the tile floor and peeked into the hallway. The flat was designed in the same layout as mine, with the kitchen off the hallway that ran from the front door to the opposite end of the flat, where two doors stood open, one to the sitting room and the other to the bedroom. All was in darkness.

The silence had an emptiness to it, the feel of absence. I thought I was alone, but it seemed prudent to check and make sure of that fact before I began looking for evidence of who lived in 228. I pushed back the curtain over the sink and let in some of the ambient light from the city. It wasn't a foggy night, and the moon was out.

I crept down the carpeted length of the hall, pausing to survey the sitting room and bedroom. Both were empty. Unlike my flat, which had white-painted walls and crown molding, every room in this flat was paneled in English oak. No wonder Minerva had never heard anything through the walls.

The drapes were open, and moonlight streamed in through the large window in the sitting room, falling across the thick ruby and gold Oriental rug and deep leather chairs. Cherrywood side tables reflected the strips of moon-light that traced across their polished surfaces. Wall sconces were set in the oak panels, but I didn't dare switch on the lights since the curtains were open. I'd have to make do with the moonlight.

The bedroom was dimmer because the window was smaller, but I could see a curtained fourposter bed with a royal blue coverlet, which I navigated around so I could peek into the bathroom. A modern tub with a curtain on a circular rod above it filled most of the space. A razor, shaving cup and brush, and toothmug were arranged on a glass shelf above the sink. I checked the luminous hands on my wristwatch. Three minutes to go.

Now that I was sure no one was home, I went to the hall. Even in the darkness it was easy to see an additional door had been added beside the kitchen door. A visitor to the flat would probably assume it was a closet, but when I twisted the knob, the door swung open silently onto a brick-walled stairwell with a set of plain wooden stairs that descended to a landing that turned back on itself, then disappeared into a black maw. I whispered, "Kudos to you, Minerva. You were right."

The stairs didn't continue higher. They dead-ended at the door I held open. They were the perfect way to remove a body from South Regent Mansions. No worrying about the lift or the painters working in the back stairs, or Evans, for that matter. Just whisk it down the private staircase and out the door to the courtyard.

As gruesome as my thoughts were, I felt a modicum of relief. The body hadn't been magically transported away.

Minerva wasn't mad or imagining things. On a more personal note, my spirits lifted with the thought that I might be able to take the stairs down to the basement. I'd certainly check and see if the door at the bottom of the stairs unlocked from this side before I crawled back into the rubbish lift. But I still had a few minutes to explore the flat.

I went back through the rooms more slowly and came away even more puzzled. There was hardly anything personal in the rooms at all. No invitations or silver-framed photographs propped up on the mantel. No books or newspapers scattered across the tables or discarded on the nightstand in the bedroom. No bathrobe hanging on the back of the bathroom door. No scent bottles on the bureau.

A few items of men's clothing hung in the large wardrobe, including a three-piece wool suit and a silk dressing gown. The drawers of a bureau contained men's shirts, socks, collars, and handkerchiefs embroidered with the initials *SWU*. In a shallow drawer at the bottom of the wardrobe, I found a peach-colored negligee along with a few bobby pins. I closed the drawer and sat back on my heels. Who lived here? Except for the clothing, the flat had the feel of a lodging room—an opulent and expensively furnished lodging room, but a lodging room, nonetheless.

I returned to the kitchen and looked through the cupboards, hoping the food delivery I'd seen might have been labeled with a name or some information. But all I found were the coffee, tea, and assorted food tins.

I went back to the sitting room and stood with my hands on my hips. There was no desk to search through for letters or papers, but there was a bookshelf. I pulled out a few of the books, opened them, then snapped them shut. No name was inscribed on the flyleaf.

My time was up, and I'd discovered absolutely nothing—well, except that a man with the initials SWU lived here . . . occasionally, it seemed. The negligee indicated a woman, so perhaps a couple? But if that were the case, there should be more women's clothing as well as scent, cosmetics, and jewelry. Perhaps the woman was an infrequent visitor.

Had some unknown woman lived here, been killed, wrapped in a rug, and carried down the stairs to the basement? Then all traces of her had been removed, except the negligee in the bottom drawer, which had been forgotten when her belongings had been swept away? I felt sick at the thought.

But that train of thought didn't make sense. How could someone miss the negligee? If someone had removed clothing from the flat, the bottom drawer of a wardrobe wouldn't have been overlooked. And if a murderer had a set of private stairs that conveniently led to the basement, why would he—or she—take the body, roll it in a rug, and position the rug in the hall of the second floor for anyone going down the lift to see? No, that didn't make sense at all. And why all the secrecy around flat 228 in the first place? Why had no one ever seen the Darkwaiths?

Frustration flared through me as I checked my watch. Time was up. I went to the door that led to the basement.

I opened it, and light flooded over me. My heart kicked, then began to beat so fast that I felt lightheaded for a moment. Every brick was picked out in the brilliant glow of a row of overhead lights that had been switched on.

I yanked the door closed, halting its quick sweep at the last second so that it didn't slam. As I eased the door into the frame, a man's voice with an upper-class accent carried up the stairwell along with the thick stomp of footsteps on the wooden treads, "Thank you, Evans. I'll ring down when we're ready for the motor."

Evans's familiar voice responded. "Very good. I'm on duty all night and—"

I couldn't see the man who was speaking to Evans. The twist in the stairs and the landing blocked my view, but I didn't want to come face-to-face with him when he turned at the landing.

I dashed for the kitchen and opened the cupboard door, not caring that I'd have to wedge myself into the rubbish lift. Minerva would lower me and—*Minerva!* I froze, one foot poised on the metal platform. Minerva had been in the basement where Evans and the unknown man had just been. If I crawled into the rubbish lift, would she be there to lower it? I couldn't count on it. I wasn't about to wait around, stuck in that small metal box, waiting to be discovered by the man who was climbing the stairs.

I shoved the cupboard door closed, dashed down the hall to the flat's main door, threw back the bolts, and stepped into the bright corridor of the second-floor hallway.

CHAPTER FIFTEEN

*T*stood on the crimson runner in the hallway for a second, trembling like Ace when he shivered with excitement as he waited for the lift gate to be pulled back. My instinct was to head for my flat and hole up there like a fox hiding from the hounds, but I had to check on Minerva. I scurried along the little hall to the back stairs. I was about halfway down the first flight of stairs when I heard someone coming up from below me, but it wasn't the typical slap of shoes on the wooden treads. The sound was softer and more muffled.

Minerva turned the corner at the landing. She looked up and saw me. "Oh, thank goodness! I didn't know how you were going to get out of the flat." She held her shoes in one hand. Splotchy stains marred her stockings and the hem of her skirt. She padded up the stairs to within a few steps of me, holding her shoes out from her body as if she didn't want them to brush against her.

"I'm fine," I said, but my voice sounded breathless. I drew

in a gulp of air. "I was inside the flat and heard a man coming up the stairs—you were right about the section of the blueprints, by the way. They're stairs, not a lift, but it *is* a private entrance to flat 228. The stairs don't continue up to the next floor. It only runs from the basement to the second floor. When I realized someone was coming up from the basement, I raced out and left through the flat's front door. Walked right out. Ran, actually. What happened to you?" I moved down a step, and Minerva put up a hand.

"Don't come closer. I'm sure I smell ghastly. The basement suddenly became as busy as Waterloo Station, so I hid in one of the big rubbish carts."

"Ugh! How unpleasant. I never thought anyone else would come down to the basement while we were there."

"Neither did I. I was standing there, holding onto the chain, counting down the seconds on my watch when I heard footfalls on the back stairs. I moved from the rubbish lifts to the darker area away from the light. It was Evans."

"I thought he stayed in the lobby during his shift."

"Not tonight."

"He didn't see you, though?"

"No. He had a set of keys in his hand, and he was focused on moving them along the ring—to find a certain key, I suppose. I wasn't sure where he was going or what he was going to do in the basement, but I couldn't get past him to leave, so I climbed into one of the carts." She winced. "It was rather disgusting." She lifted her shoes and gestured at her skirt. "Unfortunately, they were mucky."

"Let's get you back to your flat so you can change out of those things."

"All right, but I advise you to keep your distance," Minerva said as we ascended the staircase. "The smell is foul."

"So, I take it Evans didn't see you at all?"

"No. He never even looked my way. He walked up the ramp and unlocked the door to the courtyard. I stayed hunched over below the rim of the cart, but I could hear the engine of a motor as it pulled into the courtyard outside. Then I heard voices, a man's—not Evans, because the accent was posh—and a woman's. The man greeted Evans in a matter-of-fact way, like it was perfectly normal for Evans to unlock the basement door and escort him through the rubbish carts. They went to the door that was locked. Evans unlocked it, the man and woman went through, and Evans locked it back. Then he went back and locked the door to the courtyard."

We reached the second floor's brightly lit corridor, which was empty. We hurried along the crimson runner to Minerva's door. Once we were inside her flat, I said, "It's a shame you didn't see who Evans let in the building."

"Oh, but I did. I waited until I heard the group pass me, then I looked over the edge of the cart. They were all turned away from me, but the light was strong enough to see the man's profile. It was Stanley Winton Underhill." She gave each word of the man's name an equal amount of emphasis and waited for my reaction.

"That name sounds familiar, but I can't quite place it . . ."

"He's in Parliament. He was in the paper last week. I think is still have it." She found it in a stack of newspapers on the counter in the kitchen, then handed it to me. "Five or six pages in, I think. Here, let me have the front page for my shoes." She spread the newsprint on the floor and left her soiled shoes on it. "Let me change, and I'll tell you about the woman who was with him."

I sat down on the sofa in the sitting room and found the article, which described a speech that Underhill had given to his constituents. He stated that even though he held a seat in Parliament, he was "no different than a miner or a shop clerk or a lorry driver." An accompanying photograph showed Underhill shaking hands with a line of people. A woman with a toothy smile and a frizzy halo of dark hair stood at his elbow. Her build was statuesque, and her feathered hat waved in the air above her husband's head.

By the time I finished the article, Minerva, wrapped in a brocade dressing gown, handed me a glass. "It's a G & T. Thought you might need one. I certainly do." She seated herself at the opposite end of the sofa from me. "I'm afraid there will be no salvaging that skirt. The stains are too deep, but I might be able to save the shoes."

I handed her the newspaper. "A real man of the people, Underhill. He's no different from the working man."

"So he claims."

"You said you saw the woman who was with Underhill tonight. Was it . . ." I tipped my head in the direction of the paper.

Minerva glanced at the photograph. "His wife? Definitely not. I only saw the woman from the back, but the woman with Underhill tonight was shorter than him, had whitish blonde hair, and looked rather . . . well—to be perfectly honest—cheap." She sent me a look that seemed to say, *she was one of* those *sorts*.

"I see."

Minerva tossed the paper onto the coffee table. "Did you discover anything about him in the flat?"

"Hardly anything."

"How can that be?"

"Because it was practically devoid of anything personal at all." I summarized what the rooms had looked like and the monogramed handkerchiefs.

"Well, Underhill's arrival and the way Evans escorted him through the basement certainly seemed to be a familiar routine for both of them. I think we can assume it's a regular occurrence."

"Which means it's a reasonable assumption that Underhill either owns the flat or leases it," I said. "I suppose the name *Darkwaith* is listed as the resident name to prevent anyone from connecting the flat with Underhill. The article mentioned that Underhill's residence is in Mayfair, which brings up several questions."

Minerva tucked her feet up on the cushion and sipped her gin. "Yes, in particular about Mrs. Underhill."

We silently sipped our drinks until Minerva asked, "Do you think the body I saw rolled in the rug was Mrs. Underhill or another woman Underhill brought to the flat?"

"I was wondering the same thing." My thoughts skipped back to the stairway that went down to the basement. "Although it doesn't make sense that he'd put a body in a rug, then put it out in the hall."

"Yes, that would be absurd when he has his own private stairwell," Minerva allowed.

"And does Underhill bring different women to the flat," I went on, questions spinning through my mind, "or is it always the same woman?"

Minerva put down her glass and leaned forward to massage her temples. "This situation just becomes more and more complicated. Shouldn't it become simpler?"

"Don't worry. It may not feel like we're making progress, but we actually are. We're close, very close, to figuring out what happened."

"But how will we track down who's been to the flat?"

"Simple. Evans will know."

"But he won't talk."

"Now that we know *who* is using flat 228, I'm confident I can wiggle the information out of him."

The lift crawled down from the second floor, then came to a halt with a bounce at the ground floor. I'd convinced Minerva to stay upstairs. The less Evans knew about the nature of my inquiries and who I was working for, the better. I pushed back the gate and kept my pace slow, allowing Mrs. Attenborough to finish speaking to Evans. We greeted each other as she passed by me on the way to the lift.

Evans was bent over his ledger. He glanced up, then returned his attention to his notes. "Good evening, Miss Belgrave." A hint of exasperation edged his polite tone.

"Hello again. I need to speak to you about Stanley Winton Underhill and flat 228."

Evans jerked upright. From his startled movement, one would have thought someone had pulled a Christmas cracker by his ear. His glance darted up and down the lobby.

I stepped closer. "No one is within earshot. I just need the truth from you about Mr. Underhill."

"I don't know what you're talking about." His reply was automatic, but the way his gaze continued to shift across the lobby betrayed his nervousness.

"I know Mr. Underhill arrived tonight. You let him into the building, then he took the private staircase from the basement up to flat 228."

He picked up his pen. "I don't know what you're talking about."

I ignored his denial. "You were observed." Not by me, but he didn't need to know that. Sometimes the things that you don't say are the most important. "The basement has quite a few dark corners, doesn't it? One might wait and watch quietly in the dark. People coming and going would never notice."

Evans dropped the pen and rubbed his hand over his extravagant walrus-like mustache as he covered a sigh. "All right, Miss Belgrave. You figured it out. Congratulations. What do you want from me? I haven't much money."

"Don't look so miserable. I'm not going to shout it from the rooftops—or blackmail you. My interest in this is not vulgar curiosity. I told you. I'm working on a case."

His bushy eyebrows descended. "You are? I thought that was a fib you made up."

"It's the truth. I can't tell you much about my case, but I have no interest in exposing Mr. Underhill's activities unless it's absolutely necessary. And I won't announce the true occupant of flat 228 to the other residents, although their curiosity is as high as mine."

"I know it is. That's why Mr. Underhill insists on complete secrecy. I told him it wasn't a good idea. Once you try to keep something secret, it makes it much more interesting. I've seen it time and time again. It's human nature."

I agreed with him, but I didn't want to be distracted from my goal of finding out about Mr. Underhill, so I said, "How long has Mr. Underhill had the flat?"

Evans gave the lobby one more quick survey, then he leaned in. "He's the owner of the building."

I felt my eyes widen. "Really? I didn't realize."

"Nobody does. All the records say the flat belongs to Winton Darkwaith. Mr. Underhill has gone to quite a bit of trouble to make sure it's very difficult to find out he's associated with the building in any way." Evans heaved a sigh. "It feels jolly good to tell someone. It's hard on a body to keep something from everyone. Even my wife doesn't know."

"I imagine that's been difficult." Evans did look less strained now that he'd unburdened his secret.

"But I didn't tell you," he cautioned. "You figured it out on your own. I can't help that."

"No, of course not," I said, but I was still mulling over Evans' statement about Underhill disassociating himself from South Regent Mansions. "What about the purchase records and permits for South Regent Mansions? Wouldn't Underhill's name be on those?"

Evans shrugged. "I don't know about things like that. If someone has enough money, a person can hide anything."

"Indeed. Perhaps he used a business name or something of the sort." I wasn't familiar with that sort of obfuscation, but Evans was right. If someone like Underhill wanted to be incognito, he certainly had the funds to make his name vanish from the official records.

"Probably layers of protection between South Regent Mansions and his real name," Evans said. "That would be my guess, knowing him."

"It wouldn't be quite in keeping with his image as a *common man* if the word got out that he owned this service flat, not to mention the residence in Mayfair."

"Too right."

"So he only comes here occasionally with certain ... companions?"

Evans nodded. "Mondays and Fridays, those are the days I expect him."

"Does he bring his wife?"

"Never."

"Do you always see him when he arrives?"

"Oh yes. He's never had—"

Evans straightened and said good evening to Diana Finch-Ellis, who was striding through the lobby, her bias-cut silk skirt fluttering. She tilted her head and looked out from under the low brim of her chic cloche as she greeted us, but she didn't stop to talk. The doorman trailed behind her with a luggage cart that was stacked with an enormous trunk, three hat boxes, and a valise. Once they'd closed the gate on the lift, Evans continued, "Mr. Underhill has never had a key. It's one of the things that he's insisted on from the very beginning. It's a paranoia, that's what it is. He's frightened that if he carried the key to the flat on him and something happened to him—if he was injured or sick—someone would find the key and learn about his connection to South Regent Mansions."

"He doesn't have a key to the building or his own flat? I find that hard to believe."

Evans said, "It's the way things are with him. He always rings first to let me know when he'll arrive. I let him in through the basement and unlock the door to the private stairway. When he's ready to leave, he departs the same way out the basement. I lock up after he's gone."

"So you always know when he comes and goes. But what happens if you're not on duty?"

"Mr. Underhill lets me know when he wants to use the flat, and I make sure I'm on duty at those times. He's keen on keeping things—what did he call it? Oh yes, *compartmentalized*. That was it. He told me once that it's safest to not have any incriminating evidence about the flat on him."

"Those were the words he used? *Incriminating evidence?*"

Evans turned his face to the side and spoke in a confiding tone, "Wife is a bit of a Tartar, I hear. She apparently controls the purse strings in the family."

"I see. Well, from what you've told me, you'll be able to clear up the only question I have left, and then I'll leave you alone. Did Mr. Underhill or any of his . . . special friends visit flat 228 on Monday?" I knew someone had been inside the flat that day because I'd seen the food delivery had been taken inside.

Evans nodded. "Mr. Underhill called that morning and said one of his—um—friends would arrive around three."

I pointed to the ledger. "Do you have who it was written down?"

Evans looked as if I'd suggested he'd put the name on a sandwich board and paraded around the lobby with it. "Nothing in writing. That's Mr. Underhill's rule."

"Of course it is."

"But I remember that it was Monday that she came. Three is a bit early for his arrivals. That's why it stands out."

"What did she look like?"

"You saw her tonight. Small and blonde."

So it hadn't been Mrs. Underhill.

Evans said, "Mr. Underhill arrived around seven that night. They both departed early Tuesday morning."

"You're sure that *both* Mr. Underhill and the woman left? You saw each of them?"

He frowned as if I'd asked a trick question. "I spoke to Mr. Underhill on the way out, and I opened the door of the motor for the woman myself."

"And no one else visited flat 228 on Monday?"

"No. No one at all."

CHAPTER SIXTEEN

I left Evans to his ledger, frustration roiling in my stomach. A lady doesn't show excessive emotion —at least not in public. The only external sign of my inner turmoil that I allowed myself was a fierce stab at the second-floor button in the lift. I closed the gate with a clank, and as the lift ascended, worry enveloped me as thick as a London pea-souper.

I'd been so sure that we were on the right track with the private staircase. But if what Evans had told me about Underhill's coming and going from South Regent Mansions was true—and Evans' profound relief at being able to share his secret indicated he'd been honest—then Minerva and I had accounted for the whereabouts of everyone on the second floor. No one was missing.

A seed of doubt sprouted in my mind. What if Minerva had truly been mistaken about what she'd seen? She was levelheaded and sensible. Because of her nature, I'd believed her wholeheartedly, but now ... perhaps she was wrong?

I pushed the lift gate open slowly, lost in thought as I ran back through all my interactions with Minerva, then I gave myself a mental shake. This was Minerva—logical and matter-of-fact Minerva. She wasn't mad. She'd confided in me, and I'd promised to help her. I simply had to go back over everything—each tiny detail—and find whatever we'd missed. We *must* have missed something.

Despite my resolve to continue the investigation, my steps dragged down the crimson runner to Minerva's door. I dreaded telling her what Evans had said. It was a setback, and it would hit her hard. I looked longingly at the door to my flat. I'd rather brew myself a strong cup of tea and put off the conversation for a bit, but I squared my shoulders. It had to be done. I had to tell her what I'd learned.

When I knocked on her door, she flung it back, then did an about-face and hurried away from me. She'd changed into a tweed suit and held a stack of folded clothes in one arm. She called over her shoulder, "I'll let you close the door. I must keep packing if I'm to catch the train at half past."

"Train? Where you going?"

"I've just had a telephone call from one of mother's friends in the village. Mummy tripped over a tree root today on her way back from the greengrocer. She's broken her arm and has a horrible gash across her head. Twelve stitches. Can you believe it? She's disoriented and asking for me. I must go."

"Of course you must." I followed Minerva into the bedroom, where she placed the folded clothes in the corner of the suitcase, which was splayed open on her bed.

"I wouldn't worry, except she's seemed a tad forg
the last few times I've visited."

"I didn't realize. I'm sorry to hear that."

Minerva concentrated on aligning a pair of stu
walking shoes within the confines of the suitcase. "Yes, w
It's not something one shares, is it?"

Minerva disappeared to the bathroom, and her voi
echoed off the hard surfaces. "I'll bring it up with the villaꞯ
doctor while I'm there." The medicine cupboard clicked a
she opened and closed it. "I may have to bring her back t
London with me and take her to a specialist."

Minerva steamed back into the bedroom with her
dressing gown billowing around her as she swept by.
"Which is why it's so important to keep old Harrison at least
satisfied, if not happy—although, that might be impossible. I
don't think I've ever seen the man smile. Harley Street
specialists are far from inexpensive. And this means I'll miss
Harrison's dratted fiftieth birthday party, which won't help
the situation."

"He's throwing a birthday party?" From what I'd heard
about her boss, he didn't seem the type to celebrate
milestones.

She tucked her sponge bag into a gap in the suitcase,
then spread her dressing gown on the bed, smoothed out
the creases, and folded and layered it on the top of her suitcase. She tucked it down around the edges, which would
hold the contents in place. "His wife is throwing the party
for him at Rules. Mandatory attendance for the
department."

"Swanky."

"Yes. It will be a pity to miss the food if nothing else."

As she flipped the case closed and snapped the latches, any lingering doubts about her mental acuity fell away. No matter how flustered she was, her common sense and methodical nature came through, even in her packing. "I have no idea when I'll return. Hopefully in a day or so." She turned to the glass over her dressing table and jabbed a pin into her hat, then checked her watch. "I'll make the train," she said with a note of relief. "Oh!" She spun around. "The telephone call about Mummy completely swept away any thought about Evans. What did you find out?"

For a second I considered keeping my news to myself. She already had a rather heavy burden of worries, but I wouldn't want information kept from me. Aware that seconds were ticking away, I left out the part about Mr. Underhill owning the building and only gave her the most important news, describing the arrangement he had with Evans to escort him in and out of the building at his convenience.

Minerva picked up her suitcase in one hand and her handbag in the other. "How bizarre."

"I agree."

She switched off the lights in the bedroom with her elbow, then headed down the hallway to the door of her flat with me walking behind her. "Do you believe Evans?"

"I do."

She stopped and turned back. "But then that means . . . there's no one left." The expression that washed over her face was ghastly. *Devastated* was the word that popped into my mind, and that only reinforced my assur-

ance of her firm grip on reality. She really, truly believed that she had seen someone bundled up in the rug.

"No, I think it means we've missed something." I motioned for her to resume walking. "I'll simply have to go back over everything we've discovered. We must have made a mistake somewhere—overlooked something." I inched around her and opened the door for her. "The very fact that you're doubting yourself is an indication that you're not mad. Leave everything to me. I'll let you know about anything I discover."

Minerva had been in almost continual motion from the moment I'd entered her flat, but she went completely still and blew out a long breath, her shoulders moving as she exhaled. "Thank you, Olive."

"It's nothing. Now, off you go," I said as we stepped into the hall.

Minerva locked her flat and dashed for the lift, then jerked back around to me. "Olive, wait! One more thing."

I removed my key from the lock on my door as she half jogged back down the hall to me. She transferred her handbag to the same hand as her suitcase so she could reach into her pocket as she scurried along. She took out a folded piece of paper. "This is where I'll be."

The lift glided into position, the chime rang out, and Minerva reversed course, calling over her shoulder, "You can send a telegram or telephone mother's neighbor."

I tapped the note against my palm, my gaze going to Lola and Constance's flat. I still hadn't received anything from Constance about how to reach Lola. As the lift descended, I went to flat 225 and knocked. After a minute, I knocked again, more firmly.

Mrs. Attenborough's door opened, and her well-coiffed head popped out. "Please leave off, Miss Belgrave. This isn't a lodging house. If you need to speak to the young ladies who reside in the flat, kindly leave a message with Evans for them or employ the telephone. All the flats are equipped with telephones, you know."

She closed the door before I could reply. I marched back to my flat. Perhaps I closed the door a tad louder than was strictly necessary. I telephoned the flat next door, but there was no answer. I made a mental note to check with Evans to see if Constance was out or if she was avoiding me.

The carriage clock chimed, which jogged my memory about my plans with Jasper for the evening. "The theater," I squeaked and dashed to change.

CHAPTER SEVENTEEN

"*D*o hurry, Jasper," I said as we navigated through the throng of people departing the theater. "I'm sure that was Constance." Jasper's tall figure cut a swath through the crowd, and I followed along in his wake until we came out into the night air that smelled of rain. The weather had warmed a bit and the storm clouds that hovered over London had only brought rain, not snow or sleet.

The shiny cobbles reflected the headlights of the motors as they streamed by. We paused in the bottleneck immediately outside the theater doors. People swirled and eddied around us like a fast-moving stream flowing over rocks protruding from a riverbed. I popped up on my toes and surveyed the people fanning out from the theater. "She was in a maroon dress and a dark coat. Her companion had dark hair, hair parted in the middle and slicked back."

Jasper's gaze skimmed the street. "Unfortunately, that

describes at least a third of the men here, and it looks as if nearly all the women are in dark coats."

"I know it's not much help. There was something familiar about the man. At the moment I can't place where I saw him, but I will." The crowd shifted, and I caught a glimpse of Constance. She and her companion were moving away. "I see them." I waved and called, "Constance!"

Someone bumped into my shoulder, throwing me off balance. Jasper caught my other elbow as a woman said, "Terribly sorry—oh! Olive, isn't it?" Diana, in her dark full-length mink coat, stood at my elbow.

"Yes, that's right. I'm Olive Belgrave. How do you do?"

"I thought that was you, Olive. I apologize for jostling against you. I lost my footing there. These cobblestones are so slick."

"I'm fine. No harm done. Excuse me for a moment. I just saw someone . . ." I searched the outer fringe of the dispersing theatergoers, trying to locate Constance again. I spotted her as Diana said, "And Jasper! Lovely to see you, darling."

"Always a delight," Jasper said.

Constance and her companion had moved a little farther down the street. She looked over her shoulder. I popped up on my tiptoes again and waved, but Constance turned away. She tugged on her companion's arm, and he hailed a passing taxi. They climbed into it and motored away.

Constance was definitely avoiding me. I would have let out a huff of irritation, but I didn't want Diana to think it was directed at her. I squished down my exasperation and turned back to the group around Jasper, spotting a familiar face at Diana's side—Monty Park.

"Hello, Jasper, old man," he said as they shook hands.

Jasper said, "Haven't seen you in a while, Monty."

"The *mater* set me off to the hinterlands to visit family for the holidays. Got caught up in a few things there and just now made it back to town."

Diana hooked her hand through the crook of Monty's elbow. "And this is his first outing since returning to town. I'm delighted he invited me to the theater with him."

"You're always an amusing companion, Diana." Monty's words were a typical social compliment, but his warm tone and the look he gave her made me glance back and forth between the two of them.

Diana squeezed his arm. "As are you." Their gazes locked for a moment, and while they were absorbed in each other, Jasper caught my eye, then nodded up the street where I'd seen Constance.

I shook my head and mouthed the word *gone*.

Diana pulled her gaze away from Monty and said to us, "You must come back to the flat with us. It's a shame that we've never had time to properly talk, Olive. Do say you'll come."

Monty added, "Yes, do. I want to hear about your latest detective exploits. I feel that the newspapers—as salacious as they are—have omitted some details that I suspect are rather juicy."

"We're all going," Diana added. "Monty and I and"—she motioned to a couple standing a bit off to the side of our group—"Becks and Ronny as well." The woman had jet-black hair and an upturned nose. She was giggling, her head was bent close to a skinny young man with an unruly thatch of rusty red hair and a freckled complexion.

Becks looked up at her name. "What?"

"You're coming back to my flat, aren't you? And Ronny too?"

"Of course. You promised to make omelets. Wouldn't miss them for the world. Much better than going to a club. I'm bored with clubs. They're all the same—stuffy and hot and the same dances over and over again. I'd much rather have an omelet. I'm starving."

The young man with her said, "And the liquor at your place is superior. Better prices too."

Diana laughed at his quip, then said to us, "You know Becks and Ronny, don't you? Olive, this is Lady Rebecca Norton and Ronny Hildebrand."

The pair nodded as Diana turned back to Monty. "Let's go before it rains again."

I glanced at Jasper, eyebrows raised. He nodded in a *whatever you'd like* kind of way.

"Sounds marvelous. We'll meet you there?"

"Smashing." Diana climbed into the cab Monty had hailed. Becks and Ronny squished in with them.

As the taxi splashed away through the puddles, Jasper and I stepped back so our shoes wouldn't be drenched.

Jasper raised his arm to hail the next cab, and I said, "It was too good an opportunity to pass up. I've never been inside her flat. Who knows what we might find out?"

"Yes, where there's one private staircase, there might be others." On our way to the theater, I'd brought Jasper up to date on everything that had happened at South Regent Mansions after he'd left.

I playfully punched his arm. "There are no more private staircases. Minerva studied those blueprints and checked every nook and cranny. The only unaccounted for space was the one we found today." Jasper opened the door of the taxi. I climbed in and said, "And there's the omelets as well."

He gave the address and closed the door. "Yes, it's not every day that an heiress offers to make you an omelet. I do hope they're edible."

Monty wiped the corners of his mouth. "You make a jolly good omelet, Di."

Monty was right. I hadn't thought Diana would be a good cook, but she'd tied an apron on over her golden evening gown that was embroidered with seed pearls and moved about the kitchen with ease. The omelets were light and golden, studded with finely chopped tomatoes and onions and cheese oozing along the edge.

"You don't have to sound so surprised. It's practically the simplest meal one can make."

Monty raised his fork. "I beg to differ. Beans on toast. Now there's a culinary treat that anyone can make—even me. You'd be surprised how difficult cooking is for some— my man, for one. Literally can't boil an egg. I had to hire a cook."

We were seated around Diana's rosewood dining room table. I'd managed to steer the conversation away from me and my discreet detective work. The last thing I wanted was to spook Diana. Monty was savvy enough to pick up on my hesitancy to speak about my previous cases and hadn't brought up the topic after I'd dodged his first question.

I'd never been inside Diana's flat. When we arrived and moved from the gilt-framed mirrors in the entrance hall to a spacious sitting room furnished in shades of peach and cream, it struck me how little I knew of the residents of South Regent Mansions. Each flat was so different. Miss Bobbin's had felt homey and lived-in with her squashy chairs and plants and Ace jumping up on my leg to welcome me. Minerva's flat had a more utilitarian bent with her simpler furnishings and her angled desk. Diana's flat was sophisticated. The deep pile of the carpets, the gilt touches, and the expensive decor of porcelain and crystal spoke of luxury.

Diana stood and began to gather the plates.

"Let me help." I stacked Jasper's plate on mine.

"There's no need, Olive."

"I insist. I'm rather handy with the washing up."

Ronny and Becks passed their plates to me while Monty and Jasper shifted back their chairs to stand.

Diana waved them off. "I'll let Olive help me, but the rest of you are exempt. There's only room in the kitchen for one other person. Becks, why don't you put something on the gramophone? But not too loud."

CHAPTER EIGHTEEN

*a*s I followed Diana into the kitchen, she said over her shoulder to Becks, "Otherwise, I'll have Miss Bobbin angry at me again, and I've only just got back in her good graces."

I took the stack of plates and opened the cupboard door that concealed the rubbish bin, which was in the same place in all the flats. "What did you do to upset Miss Bobbin?"

"The question usually is, what *didn't* I do? I'm not sedate enough for her."

I tilted the first plate over the bin and had the knife poised to scrape it clear of toast crumbs and bits of cheese, but I paused. Diana, her back to me, turned on the faucet and raised her voice over the water, "Miss Bobbin is not fond of music at all. Especially modern music . . ."

A photograph of a man rested at the bottom of the bin, half-hidden under a piece of newspaper. It was the man I'd seen with Constance at the theater. I used the knife to edge it out. The photo had been torn in half, a jagged rip that ran down the center of the man's face. Even though half the photo was missing, one glance at the man's fleshy lips and slicked-back dark hair was enough to recognize him. He was the man I'd seen with Diana in the market town in Surrey—and I was positive the same man had been with Constance tonight.

I glanced up. Diana was removing a diamond bracelet while the water filled the sink. Using the knife blade, I flicked the photograph over. "Alec W" was penned on the back. I nudged the photograph back so that it was facing up for one more look.

She laid the bracelet on the windowsill and reached for her apron.

I ran the knife over the plate. Scraps of egg splotched onto the man's face as I realized Diana's voice had lifted at the end of the last sentence.

"Sorry, what was that? I couldn't hear over the water."

She twisted the knob to turn off the faucet. "Do you know Monty well?"

"Well, fairly well. He's not an extremely close friend, though." How does one describe the relationship that develops after a murder occurs while visiting a country house? You're certainly more than acquaintances, but I hadn't kept up with Monty since the events at Archly Manor. I sensed there was more behind the question than just a casual inquiry or an effort to make conversation. "In my book, he's a gem."

Diana nodded. "That's what I thought. *And* he passed the Lola Test."

"The Lola Test? What's that?"

Diana picked up a bundle of forks and scrubbed them. "Something Lola told me. I've thought of it as the Lola Test ever since she mentioned it. She told me Alec was no good."

The change in her voice indicated he was someone who'd lost favor with her. "Alec . . . ?" I asked.

"Alec Woodwiss." Water splashed out of the sink onto the counter as Diana plunged a plate under the suds. "A cad. A complete cad."

"Really? I don't know him."

"Steer clear of him if he comes your way, that's my advice. He's a fortune hunter."

"Nothing for me to worry about there."

Diana flushed "Oh—I didn't—"

"It's fine. I'm a working girl. No one will chase me for my money. I have enough to be comfortable—very comfortable—but nothing to attract that sort of man." A few months ago, my financial state would have been a sore spot. I'd had a rather nice inheritance set aside for me, but some investment shenanigans had removed that safety net from my life. I'd been quite resentful about it, but I'd come to terms with it, I realized. The usual ball of cold fury that used to press on my chest when I thought of it wasn't there. In fact, it hadn't been there since I'd discovered who was responsible and had a hand in making sure they didn't defraud anyone else.

I picked up a tea towel as the sounds of jazz floated through from the sitting room. "So, Lola told you something about Alec?"

Diana handed me a clean, dripping plate. "At the time, I

didn't believe her. Our discussion became rather heated. We were actually shouting in the hall. That's *another* reason Miss Bobbin is upset with me." Diana gave a sticky bit on one of the plates a vicious scouring. "Lola was entirely right about Alec."

"And she had some sort of test?"

"Yes. I didn't believe her. She said Alec had been sniffing around her—those were her exact words—for months. When she told him that she didn't have control of her money, that it was tied up with a trust and the trustees were sticklers who wouldn't authorize frivolous expenses, he disappeared. It wasn't true, the bit about the trustees. She just said it to test him."

I took the next plate from Diana. "I didn't realize Lola was that well-off."

Head bent, she looked up at me from the corner of her eye. "Her grandfather was Clark Montbank. She's his sole heir."

"Oh. Oh my."

Diana grinned. "She doesn't live like she's an heiress, does she? She doesn't splash out the way I do." She glanced down at the diamond bracelet on the windowsill. "Her ways are much quieter, but she's very well taken care of. Her parents died within a month of each other. The Spanish Flu."

"Oh, how terrible. She mentioned her mother had passed, but I didn't know her father was gone as well," I said, thinking of a day I'd helped her gather her scattered belongings.

Lola had been juggling a package as she stepped into

the lift. She'd bumped against the metal gate and hit the latch on her handbag, which popped open, causing the bag to tilt. Cosmetics and coins had rained down on the marble of the lift floor. I'd hunched over to help her pick up the scattered items and plucked a folded piece of paper from the corner where it blended with the Carrera marble.

After she'd jerked the paper from my hand, she'd immediately apologized. "Oh, I am sorry. That was rather rude. But it's the last letter I received from my mother. I was away at boarding school when she . . ." She'd trailed off and cleared her throat. "Well, she's gone now." She'd put everything back into the handbag and snapped it closed. "I keep it with me always."

"I can understand that," I'd said, thinking of my mother's pearls. If I had a letter from my mother that had been written in the last days of her life, I'd cling to that too.

I gave the plate a final wipe and stacked it on top of the others. The charities research made sense now, as did Lola's comments about tedious questions and pestering. If a charity knew the heir of Clark Montbank was making inquiries but decided she didn't want to contribute . . . well, that could be quite awkward. I had to get my report to Lola whether or not Constance found me irritating. I'd tackle that duty first thing in the morning.

Diana swished the suds around and fished out a spatula. "She thought Alec was pursuing me for my money. Lola dared me to tell him that I didn't have access to it, or that my family was in financial trouble, or that I'd be disinherited if I continued to see him. She said it didn't matter which fib I told. Once he knew there was no money to be had, he'd be shot of me within a few days."

"And you tried it?"

"Not at first. I was so angry with her. A girl likes to think a man likes her for herself, you know? Not her bank balance." Diana handed me the clean spatula. "Now I realize she was trying to help. She'd seen Alec with me in the lobby, and she wanted to warn me. I'll have to apologize to her when she returns from Scotland. I do hate eating humble pie." She wrinkled her nose. "So unsavory! But she was right. Alec and I both went to visit friends in Surrey this week. I dropped a hint that my family wasn't well-off, that we were barely hanging on financially, and Alec's manner cooled immediately. I told him Tuesday. He had a sudden message and had to return to London on Wednesday morning. That was the last I've heard of him. He hasn't been in touch since."

"I'm sorry."

"No. Better to know now." She wiped the sink and counter with the dishcloth, then draped it over the faucet. She dried her hands on a towel. "I decided all men must pass the Lola Test. I tried it on Monty tonight, and do you know what he said?"

"I can't imagine." I had no idea if Monty was well-off or not. It was often hard to tell. One could put up a good front to a point. I'd done it myself when my funds vanished.

Diana took off the apron. "It didn't faze him. He said, 'It's fine, old thing. I've already purchased the tickets for tonight. I wasn't going to touch you for them.'"

We shared a laugh and returned to the sitting room. The

peach, cream, and pale blue carpet had been rolled up. Becks and Ronny were dancing while Jasper and Monty conversed by a window, blowing smoke from their cigarettes out through the open casement. Jasper snuffed his out and came across to me. "Care to dance?"

"Sounds lovely."

CHAPTER NINETEEN

I stepped into Jasper's arms, and we set off in a lively quickstep. When that song ended, Monty put on a waltz, and Jasper and I made sweeping loops around the sitting room at a slower pace. He tilted his head to my ear and spoke, his voice barely above the music. "It appeared you were having quite a tête-à-tête with Diana in the kitchen."

"She told me about an argument she and Lola had. Miss Bobbin overheard their raised voices but didn't know what they were arguing about. Now I know the full story. Lola was warning Diana about a cad."

"Not Monty, surely? He's straight." Jasper looked across the room to where Monty and Diana were dancing, their attention focused on one another.

"No, someone else. Alec Woodwiss. But that hardly seems to matter at this point. She and Monty are getting along swimmingly. Unfortunately, I didn't get to ask her about any strange goings-on here at South Regent Mansions."

"But you've added another detail to your treasure trove of facts."

I grinned. "I like that, treasure trove of facts—although I only have Diana's side of the story. It did seem as if she was being truthful, though. Her story of her argument with Lola didn't show her in a flattering light."

"It appears she's moved on from the cad." Jasper said, eyeing Diana and Monty. They were deep in conversation as they swirled around the sitting room.

"What Diana told me may be helpful. It may not. When one is in the midst of a case, it's so hard to tell which of the small details are the critical ones. After all, what I thought was vitally important, the identity of the occupant of flat 228, turned out to be a dead end."

"Yes, but you've eliminated him as being involved."

"I suppose so."

"Don't sound so grudging. You're too hard on yourself. You are making progress."

"Such good progress that I eliminated everyone on the second floor," I said, allowing a small smile. "I intend to go back over the case tomorrow. I'll comb through every detail. Hopefully, I'll find something I overlooked or discounted."

We fell silent, and Jasper pulled me closer as we twirled. I shifted my thoughts away from Minerva and the rolled-up carpet. Jasper had been kind enough to invite me to a play, which was a much sought-after ticket in London. I didn't want him to think I hadn't enjoyed it. I relaxed into the dance and only thought about how nice Jasper's hand felt on the small of my back and how wonderful it was to be so near him and feel the muscles of his arm flex under the fabric of the tailcoat. I pulled back a bit and said, "*The End of the Line* was quite entertaining. I can see why it's so popular. The leading lady did very well, but I couldn't help but think how much Miss Ravenna would have enjoyed the role."

"The same thought occurred to me," Jasper said.

"Any word from Miss Ravenna?" I'd met the famous actress when I stayed at a country house over Christmas. "I saw a newspaper article that said she's stopping over in a German spa."

"The newspapers are a bit off, as usual. I had a note from her a few day ago. It was posted from Munich. She's having a lovely time. Nothing but the usual public pleasantries."

Becks and Ronny were doing the deep-kneed steps of the tango, despite the fact that the music was a waltz. They cut across the room on a diagonal, and we had to dodge out of their way. They reached the other side of the room and broke apart. Becks leaned against the wall as she giggled, then straightened and drew a shaky breath. "Again!" she said, and they were off, slanting across the room, arms outstretched, cheeks pressed together.

Jasper spun us out of their way to a far corner of the room. "Back to your adventure in the Darkwaiths' flat," he said. "I'm quite put out that you launched into breaking and entering without me. It was my idea, after all."

"I would have loved to have included you—although I know you wouldn't have enjoyed the basement. It was rather filthy. Poor Minerva got the worst of it, having to hide in the rubbish carts."

"Yes, you did spare me Grigsby's wrath. I am thankful for that."

"You're welcome. Minerva and I seized the moment. Besides, the rubbish lift was extremely small. I was the only one who would fit in it."

"You'd be surprised what a contortionist I am." The skin around his eyes crinkled as he grinned, but then the laughter left his face. "It was quite risky, what you did. This business with Underhill . . ." Jasper broke off, but I could tell that he had more to say.

"Do you know him?"

"Not extremely well. I've made up numbers for Mrs. Underhill at her dinner parties. I've spoken to Underhill occasionally at the club, but one hears things. He's ruthless. You don't want to make an enemy of him."

"No need to worry on that count. Evans swears that both Underhill and the woman with him left alive."

"And Mrs. Underhill?"

My steps slowed. "That is a loose thread. It did cross my mind, and Minerva's as well, that Mrs. Underhill might be the victim. Of course, after what Evans told me, I don't see how that could be."

Jasper matched the pace of his steps to mine. "Best to make sure."

"Yes, I shouldn't just take Evans' word."

"Mrs. Underhill is involved in all sorts of charities," Jasper said. "She spends most of her days in committee meetings. I can check on that for you."

"Would you?"

"Yes, of course. My Watson-ing duties have been quite light lately, so it's no problem at all."

"Thank you, that would be wonderful."

"I'll tackle it first thing tomorrow."

"Excellent. While you do that, I'll re-examine all the facts Minerva and I have gathered about the residents of South Regent Mansions." Once that was settled, I rested my head on his shoulder. We danced the rest of the evening and didn't talk about the case again.

Despite my late night, I awoke before sunrise and got to work straightaway. It was another gloomy day with dark clouds hanging low. I brewed a cup of coffee and jotted down what Diana had told me about Alec and Lola. Then I spent the morning double-checking my notes and typing them up. I'd hoped that the change in format from hand-writing to typed text would highlight something new, a small detail that I'd missed. And I'd also thought that perhaps my brain would work on the problem while I typed. Maybe an indirect approach to the situation—sideways rather than straight on—might give a new result. But when I surveyed my notes after a few hours, the only discovery I made was that I was still far from proficient in touch typing.

I heard the faint thud of a door closing and recognized it as coming from the flat next door. I popped up. "Oh, shoot!" After speaking to Diana last night, I was determined to get an address out of Constance so I could send my report about the charities on to Lola. When I began working this morning, it had been too early to knock on Constance's door, so I'd planned to work for an hour or so, then take a break and go around to her flat later. But I'd been so deeply occupied with my notes that I'd completely lost track of time.

I flew out of the flat and caught a glimpse of Constance from the waist up as the lift descended below the level of the floor. I reversed course and headed for the stairs. When I emerged in the lobby and looked through the rain-streaked glass doors, Constance was settling herself in a taxi. By the time I crossed the lobby, the taxi had blended into the traffic halfway down the road.

Frustrated, I decided a break was in order. I returned to my flat to collect my coat, hat, gloves, handbag, and umbrella. I set off to the tea shop a few blocks away. The Chelsea buns were fresh out of the oven, and I consumed one along with a strong cup of tea. I was striding along the pavement on my way back to South Regent Mansions, rain pattering on my umbrella, when someone called my name.

Miss Bobbin approached in a thick fur coat that swallowed her slender form, an open umbrella in one hand and Ace's lead in the other. The terrier strained at the end of the lead, delighted to encounter a friend.

"Miss Belgrave, do you have a moment?"

"Hello, Ace." I stroked the terrier's damp back and gave his ears a rub. He stopped moving for a moment, closed his eyes, and tilted his head back, leaning into my hand. "Yes, of course."

She juggled the umbrella and dog lead with ease as she

opened her handbag and took out an envelope. "I'm hosting a little bridge party on Sunday evening. I do hope you'll attend. I'm inviting everyone on the second floor as well as some of my bridge students."

"Sounds delightful. Thank you for the invitation."

As she reached to close her handbag, she said more to herself than to me, "Oh, bother."

"Anything wrong?" I asked.

"Nothing important. I meant to drop Mr. Culpepper's invitation off on my way out, but I forgot."

"I'm returning to my flat. I'll be happy to do that for you."

"Would you?"

"Yes, it's no problem at all." I didn't mind running the small errand for Miss Bobbin, and it would let me check on Mr. Culpepper. It wasn't that I didn't trust Minerva, but I wanted to see him for myself. Delivering the note was the perfect opportunity to do so.

A few minutes later, I knocked briskly on Mr. Culpepper's door, hoping I'd catch him before he left for his office.

The door swung open, and the words I'd prepared to say about passing on the invitation from Miss Bobbin flew out of my mind. It looked as if Mr. Culpepper had three hands, but then I realized he was holding a prosthetic.

"Oh my!" The words popped out before I could stop them.

"I startled you. I apologize, Miss Belgrave." He pushed his glasses up the bridge of his nose with his index finger.

"No worries. It's fine, just a little unexpected." I held out the envelope. "I just met Miss Bobbin on her way out of the building. She forgot to give this to you. I offered to drop it off since I was on my way in. It's an invitation to a bridge party."

"Oh." He'd been reaching for the envelope—with his own hand, not the prosthetic—as I spoke, but when I said the word *bridge*, his movement slowed. "It's been years since I played."

"I think you'll find it quite entertaining. Miss Bobbin is inviting everyone on the second floor."

Mr. Culpepper's gaze darted behind me. "Everyone?"

Did he look at Minerva's door? That was interesting.

"That's what Miss Bobbin said."

He took the envelope and tapped it against the back of the prosthetic. "I might drop in."

"I'm sure Miss Bobbin will be pleased to see you there." I gestured to the hand. "Is this one of your inventions?

"I'd hardly call it an invention. More a modification of an existing device. Friend of mine was injured in the war. I'm trying to help him out."

"It's very lifelike."

"That's the idea. He has a prosthetic with different extensions he can switch out for various tasks at his work— he's a motor mechanic—but the wooden hand he uses for social situations is a bit clumsy and doesn't look like a real hand. I'm experimenting with different materials to see which looks most realistic. This one is made of Bakelite. It's heavier than I'd like, but I may be able to reduce the weight in the next version."

A large section of the smooth, pale yellow plastic had been shaped like the palm of a hand. The fingers and thumb were made of smaller jointed pieces that flexed and moved as he shifted the piece around so I could see it from all sides.

"This is amazing. Did you make it yourself?"

"No. I know a chap who works in a factory in the States. I sketch out a diagram, and he molds the pieces. I'm working on the internals as well."

He pulled on a strap attached to the hand, and the fingers closed on the palm in a gripping motion.

"How incredibly clever."

"Thank you, but replicating movements in prosthetics is nothing new. Quite a few advancements have been made since the end of the war. In the future, there will be even more innovations, I'm sure. Eventually, we'll have replacement parts, as it were, not only for limbs, but also for other things, even organs."

"Really? That sounds rather impossible."

"Oh, no, not at all. In Germany and America, they're doing some interesting experiments right now related to the heart, lungs, and kidneys." He broke off, and pink suffused his face. He'd been swept up in the details of scientific advancements and just realized he'd raised an indelicate topic. One didn't discuss the functions of the body.

To rescue him from the awkwardness, I focused on the hand. "Well, you've done an excellent job here. In fact, if I saw it—just glanced at it—I might have mistaken it for the real thing. Are you working on any other prosthetics ... perhaps one for the foot?"

"Oh, no. This is my only focus. There's much room for improvement here." As he spoke, he moved the thumb back and forth. "See how the movement of the thumb is limited?

I'd like to get more range there, and it needs to move more smoothly."

His glasses had slipped down his nose, but he didn't push them back up. I recognize the abstract look that came over his face as he focused on the prosthetic. It was an expression that I'd seen on my father's face quite often when an idea struck him and he hurried off to his study. I knew that our conversation was at an end, but I thought I might as well try to get a little more information out of him. "I understand you're just returned from Edinburgh?"

He looked up and seemed surprised to see me still there.

"Edinburgh?" I prompted. "You're just back?"

"Edinburgh, yes. That's right. Quick journey."

"And you took the Flying Scotsman?" He nodded. "Did you happen to see anyone that you knew on the journey?"

"No. I spent the whole time preparing to meet with a client of the firm."

"I see." His gaze was open, and he didn't seem at all concerned or even curious about why I was asking. Either he was a skilled liar, or he was telling me the truth. He looked back down at the prosthetic and tugged on the thumb. Whatever idea he'd just had to improve the design took priority over any train trip or meeting anyone on said train.

"Don't forget about the invitation." I motioned to the envelope, which he'd tucked into his jacket pocket.

"Right. Yes." He patted all his pockets, found the envelope, and removed it. He saluted me with the envelope as he said, "Good day, Miss Belgrave." He closed the door, his head already dipped back over the prosthetic.

The telephone was ringing when I returned to my flat. I hurried across the room and snatched up the receiver without bothering to go around my desk.

"Hello, old bean," Jasper said. "I hope it's not too early for you?"

"Not at all. I've been up for hours."

"Sadly, I have as well, and I have news for you. Mrs. Underhill is presiding over the meeting of the Committee for the Investigation of Clairvoyance, the Unseen, and Other Phenomena as we speak."

"Blast," I muttered, then immediately felt a surge of shame. "That was rather ugly of me. I'm glad the woman is alive, but I really don't know where to go from here." I moved around to the proper side of my desk. I picked up my pencil and put a line through her name as I dropped into my chair. "Well, at least that loose end is tied up."

I swiveled in my rolling chair away from my paper-covered desk so that I faced the window. The gray day matched my mood. Soft, steady rain continued to fall, pattering against the glass.

"Yes, Mrs. Underhill is full of vim and vigor. I had a difficult time escaping her committee clutches."

"Committee clutches?" I felt a smile forming. I could always count on Jasper for an entertaining turn of a phrase.

"She was quite determined that I should attend the committee meeting with her, but I was able to extricate myself with the promise of a donation."

"To the clairvoyance committee?"

"No, to another of her causes, the Ladies Society for Aid to Blind and Maimed Soldiers."

"Well done, you."

"Thank you. Although, Grigsby was rather displeased with the state of my trousers when I returned to my lodgings. The cuffs were soaked through. I had to stroll Mayfair for half an hour this morning so that I could catch her as she left her town house. Surprising number of puddles for such an exclusive address. One would think the pavements would be smoother."

"I'm sorry that Grigsby is upset." Jasper's gentleman's gentleman wasn't enthusiastic about my friendship with Jasper. I hoped that Jasper hadn't mentioned that I was the cause of his damp trousers. "I appreciate your sartorial sacrifice."

"All in the line of duty. No other news?"

"No." I spun back to the desk and shuffled my pages of notes into a stack. The envelope with my report for Lola still sat on the corner of my desk. "I wasn't so lucky in tracking down my quarry. I missed speaking to Constance this morning by just a few moments. I may have to go to Montford's—Constance works there—to run her to ground and ask again for Lola's address in Edinburgh. It's becoming absurd. I feel as if I'm playing a game of cat and mouse with Constance."

"It is rather unusual, the way she continually puts you off. Perhaps Lola didn't go to Edinburgh. What if she went somewhere else?"

"If she did, why wouldn't Constance tell me? There's no need for secrecy. Lola can travel wherever she chooses. In any case, Lola did go to Edinburgh. The waiter on the train remembered her."

"Which meal was it?"

I replayed the conversation in my mind. "Breakfast. He said she had eggs, toast, and coffee."

"That doesn't mean she stayed on the train all the way to Edinburgh."

I'd been lounging back in the chair, using one toe to rotate the chair from side to side. At his words, I sat up straight, my feet hitting the floor. "Jasper, what an interesting thought! The waiter didn't say she returned for lunch. If she only had breakfast, then she might have gotten off the train in York." A pulse of excitement beat inside me.

"And gone somewhere else besides Edinburgh."

"Which would mean Constance is covering for her." I shuffled my notes until I came to the paper with the details about flat 225 and skimmed over typed lines with a new perspective, but nothing new had popped out at me. I dropped the page back onto the desk. "But if that's the case, why the subterfuge?"

"No idea. You said Lola was involved with the fortune hunter—what was his name?"

"Alec." I picked up a pencil and lightly underlined his name in my notes on the page with information about Lola. "Alec Woodwiss."

"The name's not familiar."

"I don't know him either." I shifted my chair closer to the desk. "Constance seems determined to avoid me, and I'm pretty sure the man I saw her with last evening at the theater was Alec Woodwiss." I drew a line across the typed page connecting the names of Alec, Lola, and Constance as my thoughts flew. The lines made a triangular shape, and that bothered me.

"Olive, are you still there?"

"Sorry, yes. Just lost in my thoughts."

"About Alec?"

"Yes, but also about Lola and Constance. I only have Constance's word that Lola went to Edinburgh. She said Lola received a telegram and departed. I know Lola was on the train from the waiter's description, but if Lola got off the train at York, her destination might be somewhere else."

"Rotten luck that you're dependent on the elusive Constance to find out where Lola went."

"Yes, and I'm beginning to suspect that Constance is being less than honest with me." I tapped the pencil point on the page, then I went still. "The telegram," I muttered.

"What was that?"

"The telegram," I repeated. "There may be a way to find out if Constance is telling the truth about Lola going to Edinburgh." I put the pencil down. "I need your help. Can you come over to South Regent Mansions as quickly as possible?"

"Always at your service, old bean."

"You're a brick, Jasper. I do hope you don't balk at this, though. I have an idea. To confirm this supposition or eliminate it, I need to get into flat 225, and there's only one way to do it."

"Why do I feel another spot of breaking and entering coming on?"

CHAPTER TWENTY

*I*n the basement of South Regent Mansions, I pushed open the metal door and showed Jasper the platform of the rubbish lift.

Jasper's forehead wrinkled as he studied the small space. "You're right. I wouldn't fit in there."

"That's why I'm the one who will go up, and you'll stay here and pull this chain." I demonstrated how the chain moved the platform. The rubbish bin from the first floor descended into view, and Jasper removed it. As I pulled the chain, the next rubbish bin appeared as the platform from the second floor came to rest on top of the one from the first floor.

Jasper removed the bin, which contained an empty champagne bottle and discarded boxes from Harrods Food Hall. "Someone had a party." He set it aside, then switched places with me.

I paused, foot poised to step into the lift. "Ready?" I

didn't want to spend any more time in the small metal space than was absolutely necessary.

"Not at all." Jasper wrapped the chain around his forearm and gripped the metal links. I hated to think what Grigsby would have to say about the sleeves of his suit coat later today. "It does seem like a frightful lot of work to search for a telegram that's probably already been tossed out."

"I know, but I *must* make the effort. This is the last thing I can think of to do to help Minerva. Everyone else on the second floor is accounted for. I've seen them myself—except for Underhill, but both Minerva and Evans saw him. Something's off with Constance. Her note said Lola received a telegram, which prompted her to leave London. If I can find the telegram, I'll know Constance told me the truth. If I draw a blank, then Constance may have lied. Then either Minerva will have to go to the police and trust that they believe her, or she'll stay quiet and wonder for the rest of her life about her sanity."

"Not something one wants to wrestle with," Jasper said, his tone resigned. "You're sure Constance is not at home?"

"Positive. I watched her leave this morning, and I confirmed with Evans that she hasn't returned."

Jasper tested the chain, and the platform inched up. He moved it back to its lowest point. "Doesn't that poor man get a day off?"

"Normally, he wouldn't be in today, but Burns is ill."

"I see. Well, Constance could have run out to the shops. She might be back at any moment."

"No, she wasn't going shopping. Before she disappeared

from my view in the lift, she was shrugging into her coat. She was in her work clothes—a plain white shirt and dark skirt. I'd say we safely have several hours before she returns."

"I don't know about you, but I'd prefer not to wait around here for an hour, and I don't want you in that flat for that long."

"Don't worry, I won't dawdle. Hearing Underhill come up the stairs when I was in his flat took several years off my life. I don't want another fright like that. I'll be as quick as possible. And the rubbish collection happens before eleven each day, so we must be out of here before the workmen arrive to empty the bins. Shall we say you'll lower me back down in a quarter hour?"

"How about ten minutes?" Jasper countered.

Jasper was usually an easygoing chap, but I could tell he wouldn't budge on the time frame. He was helping me get into the flat, so I decided not to argue. "All right."

He pushed his pristine white cuff back to check his watch and left a black smudge on it. We compared watches, the illuminated hands standing out in the dimness.

"It's five after now." I drew a deep breath of the basement's slightly purer air before I climbed into the unpleasant atmosphere of the rubbish lift. "I'll be back inside at a quarter past on the dot."

"I still don't like it, and I would rather it be me than you, but I can see that you're determined to do this. I know if I don't help you now, you'll recruit someone. You'd probably call Gwen up from the country and have her over here this afternoon to help you."

"I'm not exactly chuffed with the idea either, but once I've done this, I'll have done absolutely everything possible to help Minerva." I ducked my head so it didn't press against the ceiling of the rubbish lift. It felt slightly less claustrophobic that way. "All set."

"I'm going on record here that I still have rather large misgivings about this, but here goes." Jasper nodded and heaved on the chain. The last words I heard before the platform surged into the pitch black were, "Go quickly."

CHAPTER TWENTY-ONE

*T*he platform gave a little jerk, hung in the air for a second, then flew upward. With Jasper pulling on the chain, I barely had time to feel anxious as I zoomed through the section of pitch blackness that indicated I was passing the ground floor lobby. A thin stream of light that indicated the first-floor flat flashed by, then the lift halted with a gentle bounce at the second floor. I waited a few seconds, ear to the cupboard door, but there was no noise coming from flat 225. I pressed on the panel. The magnetic latch disengaged with a soft click. The sound seemed to echo through the apartment. I pushed the cupboard door open an inch.

Stacks of dirty dishes rose out of the sink in tilting towers. A dish rag lay crumpled on the floor. I eased the door fully open and extracted myself, then I stood and listened. The faint tick of the radiator filtered through the silence. A quick look around confirmed that Constance wasn't much of a housekeeper, which raised my spirits. The telegram might not have been tidied away. Now that I was standing, I could see that plates with crusty bits of food were scattered on the counter, and bright yellow droplets of dried egg yolk dotted the hob.

Moving on tiptoe, I left the kitchen and glanced into the sitting room, the two bedrooms, and the bath. All were empty. A knot of tension in my chest relaxed, but I still walked as silently as possible.

I went back to the sitting room for a slower survey. I'd been hoping for a desk—preferably with the telegram open on the blotter—but I wasn't that lucky. Not only was there no telegram, but there wasn't even a desk in the room.

A sturdy couch upholstered in a deep russet along with a leather chair sat in front of the fireplace on a russet and black rug. A small round table with an arrangement of wilting flowers was positioned at the opposite end of the sitting room. The only other furnishings in the room were a radio cabinet and a gramophone. Other than a few records near the gramophone and a dusting of crumbs on the table, there was nothing out of order in the sitting room, not even any invitations propped up on the mantel.

The nearest bedroom was done in the same practical, no-frills style as the sitting room. It was located at the front of the flat and had an excellent view of the park. A bed with a white coverlet stood in the middle of the room. The headboard was cherrywood with triangular inlays of a lighter wood in a geometrical pattern. A vanity table, also in cherrywood with the same pattern of inlays, sat to one side of the bed. A row of scent and cosmetics bottles was aligned against the glass. On the other side of the bed sat a small secretary desk, its flat panel opened to form a desktop. Unlike the highly varnished headboard and vanity, the desk's surface was duller and scuffed. A silver-framed photo perched on the desk's narrow top. I recognized a younger Lola, smiling as she stood between a man and woman I supposed were her parents, confirming that I was in Lola's room.

The inside of the desk was as tidy as the room. Letters were stacked in cubbyholes. I fanned them out. All of them were addressed to Dolores Mallory. None of them were from Scotland. The rest of the cubbyholes contained stamps, blank note cards, and envelopes.

I moved down the hall to Constance's room. It was as messy as the kitchen. The bed was unmade with the sheets and blanket in a tangled heap. I recognized the plain long-sleeved white shirt and crumpled dark skirt that had been tossed over a straight-backed chair in the corner. It was the work attire of all the shop girls at Montford's Department Store. Constance probably had several versions of the outfit so she could swap between them.

The closet door stood open, revealing a mound of fabric on top of the shoes that appeared to be tossed in randomly. A few dresses hung unevenly on the hangers, either sloping to the floor or pitching to the ceiling. There was no desk, and the small table beside the bed had no drawers and held only a lamp, an alarm clock, and a carafe with about half an inch of water. However, the vanity table was crowded with a jumble of brushes, scent bottles, and cosmetics along with several letters, which were propped up against the glass. I checked my watch. Five minutes left.

I made my way over to the dressing table, stepping over a dressing gown that had slipped from the end of the bed. I flipped through the letters, which were still in their envelopes and stirred up a cloud of face powder. All were addressed to Constance, and no telegram was tucked in among them. The two drawers in the dressing table contained more cosmetics.

I stood back and surveyed the room one more time, frustration percolating inside me. Had I squished myself into the rubbish lift for no reason? I turned to go, but then a glimpse of mint green by the closet caught my attention. The bright color contrasted with the splayed fringe of a black shawl that had fallen on the floor, partially hiding the color. I frowned. It was exactly the color of Lola's coat.

I picked my way through the discarded clothes that littered the floor, then crouched and twitched back the fringe. I stared for a long moment at the distinctive white feathers curling around the brim of the mint-green hat, my heart fluttering too fast. I looked up and ran my gaze over the clothes on the hangers, then reached up to pull the ones closest to me aside. At the far end of the rail, the matching pale green coat swung gently back and forth. A coldness settled on me.

"This is so wrong," I whispered as I stood. I stilled the rocking hanger, my mind ticking along, recalibrating what I knew, shifting those facts from one paradigm into another. I'd thought Lola had taken the train to Edinburgh. The waiter on the Flying Scotsman confirmed that a woman dressed in a coat and hat in the distinctive color of mint green had dined on the train, but Lola's coat was hanging in

Constance's closet. Could Constance also have a mint-green coat? But I'd never seen her in anything but dark colors.

I searched for the label on the coat. "Jeanne Lanvin, Paris Unis France," I read aloud in a reverent tone. I straightened the shoulders of the coat so that it hung evenly on the hanger and smoothed the lapels. The exquisite craftsmanship revealed itself in the subtle embroidery on the cuffs and collar as well as in the cut of the coat itself with its circular flared skirt. My feeling of dread deepened. Constance with her shop-girl salary couldn't afford something like this. And it didn't go with the rest of Constance's clothes.

Her wardrobe consisted of dark, somber colors like black, brown, and russet. The green coat seemed to glow in contrast to the funereal colors hanging on the rail and mounded on the floor. Had Lola returned from Edinburgh and lent the coat to Constance? It didn't seem likely. Lola's room had a deserted air as if no one had used it in a few days. And it had been days and days since I'd heard the faint cadence of two female voices that sometimes carried through the wall from this flat to mine next door. Another scenario spun through my thoughts—a more sinister explanation.

I repositioned the hangers as they were, put the door back at the exact angle it had been open, then backed away. I left the room with a feeling of distaste bordering on nausea coming over me as I returned to Lola's bedroom. I went to the closet and shifted through the clothes. No mint-green coat hung from the railing, and none of the hat boxes contained a cloche in that color.

I wanted to get out of the flat, but I forced myself to go slowly and be thorough. If I was right . . . well, this was probably my only opportunity to confirm my suspicions. I went to Lola's secretary desk. A small flat drawer contained a leather-bound address book with Lola's initials on the front picked out in gold.

A clock in the flat struck the quarter hour. I jumped, bobbled the address book, and dropped it on the desk. I drew a shaky breath. I'd forgotten the time. A quick check of my watch showed that the clock in the flat was two minutes fast compared to my watch. I paged through the address book, skimming the entries, forcing myself to go slow enough to study each one individually. None of the addresses listed were in Scotland, and none were in Edinburgh.

I replaced the address book and closed the flat panel, pausing for a second to look at the smiling girl in the silver frame, my heart sinking. "Oh, Lola, what's happened to you?"

CHAPTER TWENTY-TWO

*A*s I turned to leave the bedroom, I was all set to dash through the flat because I knew the moments were ticking down, but the sight of an alligator handbag hooked on the back of Lola's door stopped me in my tracks.

I stared at it for a moment, the sinking sensation in the pit of my stomach giving way to a full-on seasick feeling. The narrow clutch bag with brass hardware dangled from the doorknob. Every time I'd seen Lola, she'd had the handbag's slender strap across her wrist. Conscious of the time slipping away, I forced my feet to move.

I lifted it off the knob, the supple leather soft under my fingers. I swiveled the shiny brass catch. The inside was lined in champagne-colored silk. I tilted it side to side to have a look at the few items in the bag: a lipstick, a powder puff, a few coins, and a latchkey. A piece of cream-colored paper was tucked into the single interior pocket. I inched it out enough to see that it was a letter. I went cold all over, but I knew I had to open it.

I gently pried the folds back. The creases were worn and soft, and the swooping handwriting was faded. The salutation read, *Dearest Delores*. I turned the page over. The last words were, *Love, Mummy.* The hair on the back of my neck prickled as it stood straight. It had to be the letter Lola had snatched out of my hand when I helped her retrieve her belongings from the floor of the lift. My fingers shook so badly that it took two attempts to refold the delicate paper and place it back in the pocket. I hooked the handbag over the doorknob and rushed through the flat. I didn't want to stay a moment longer. Something horrible had happened here.

I sprinted through the flat and climbed back into the rubbish lift. It shook with my weight, and I barely closed the cupboard door before the platform began to lower. I descended as quickly as I'd risen, and in a moment, I was climbing out of the lift in the basement.

Jasper reached to help me out, and I gripped both his arms above the elbow to steady myself, not caring about any grease or dust from the chain that might be on his sleeves. He took one look at my face and said, "You've had a shock."

"You were right. Lola didn't go to Edinburgh."

Jasper handed me a cup of tea. "Drink this."

"Thank you, but I think I need something stronger."

"All in good time. Tea first."

"I suppose you're right. Better to keep a clear head."

We were inside my flat, and Jasper had interrupted my

pacing in the sitting room to hand me the cup and saucer. He'd been knocking around in the kitchen, but I'd hardly noticed as I walked back and forth in front of the large window, my thoughts in a jumble.

I lifted the teacup to my mouth, then pulled it away. "I just don't see how what I found can mean anything except the absolute worst for Lola." When I realized the letter in the handbag was from Lola's mother, all my doubts about whether or not Lola had gone somewhere else besides Edinburgh disappeared like steam coming off a boiling pot. I was sure of it now.

Jasper shifted his glance to the cup. "Tea first."

"You sound rather like my old headmistress," I said, but I obediently took a gulp. Jasper nodded and returned to the kitchen.

"I don't care if I sound like your nanny." His voice floated down the hall. "You must drink it. It'll help with the shock."

The liquid was hot and burned my tongue, but it was sweet. It warmed me at my core, and I felt some of the shivery coldness leave me as I took another slower sip.

Jasper returned from the kitchen, carrying a tray with the teapot and another cup. He set the tray down, poured a cup for himself, and took a seat on one of the chairs that flanked the sofa.

As I raised the cup to my lips, I said, "Thank you, Jasper. I do appreciate you looking after me."

"Don't mind at all, old thing. In fact, I'd quite enjoy this domestic scene—if it weren't for the possibility of what sounds like rather horrific things happening next door."

"Quite."

"Now that you've had some tea, tell me all about the clothes and handbag. I'm not clear on the details."

"Not surprising. I suppose what I was saying on the way up from the basement was a bit incomprehensible."

"I did get the gist of it. You think the presence of the green coat and hat along with the handbag add up to murder."

"I don't see anything else that it could mean." I returned the cup to the saucer, my stomach lurching. "I'm afraid it was Lola wrapped in the carpet."

"That's quite a supposition."

I paced to the window. The rain had cleared out, and now patchy clouds dotted the sky, their shadows stippling the facades of the buildings across the street and splashing gray patches across the bare trees in the park. Small figures hurried back and forth on the pavement, and motors cruised along the street, the sun flashing off the windscreens. My world had tilted at a crazy angle. It was jarring to look out and find such a normal scene.

"It's the only thing that makes sense. Why would her extravagantly expensive coat and hat, along with her favorite handbag, be in the flat next door when she's supposedly in Edinburgh?"

"Perhaps Constance liked the coat and hat so much that she bought those for herself?"

"Not on her salary. She's not an heiress like Lola. Constance works at a shop. All the other clothes in her wardrobe were plain and utilitarian. Nothing extravagant there at all."

"Then perhaps Lola has returned, and she's lent them to Constance."

"That's possible, but Lola's room felt as if no one had been in it for days. And again, why the subterfuge? Why avoid me? It's not as if I'm a pushy salesman or a persistent suitor. I'm trying to fulfill a task that Lola hired me to do. Why would she keep away from me?"

I shook my head as I put my teacup and saucer on the windowsill. "I know there are other possibilities—someone could have bought the coat and hat for Constance, or she could have borrowed them from Lola. But none of those explanations hold up when one adds in the fact that Lola's handbag is still in the flat and that it contains a letter that she told me she kept with her at all times." I stared out the window, but I wasn't seeing the busy scene below. I was thinking of the silent flat and the way the hairs on the back of my neck had prickled when I opened the letter and saw the words *Love, Mummy.* "It can only mean one thing."

I dropped down onto the sofa and rested my elbows on my knees and my forehead in my palms.

"Lola may have bought a new handbag," Jasper said, his voice soft. "Perhaps she meant to move the letter to the new bag but forgot."

"And left behind her latchkey?" I looked at him from under my hand, my head still tilted forward. "And don't say she has two keys. Because we're getting further and further down the chain of possibilities."

Jasper slid his cup and saucer onto the tea tray. He leaned forward and rested his elbows on his knees, his posture mirroring mine. "All right, let's say it *was* Lola wrapped up in the carpet. You think it was Constance who . . ."

"Murdered Lola." I straightened at his academic tone. "You're a good egg, Jasper."

He raised an eyebrow at the sudden swerve in the conversation. "I don't follow."

"You're not humoring me. You're seriously considering my position."

"Of course I'm seriously considering your position. Good gad, woman. You're brainy. Always have been. I was playing devil's advocate a moment ago. One must test one's theories, don't you know."

I couldn't help smiling back at him as he grinned at me. "And that's why you're a good egg," I said.

"Excellent. I'm happy to be 'a good egg,' although I aspire to bee's knees status in your estimation. Now, where were we?"

The brief feeling of lightness that came over me when Jasper and I bantered back and forth fell away, and I turned serious. "Constance." I blew out a breath. "I think Constance killed Lola. They shared a flat. If Lola is missing and murdered, then Constance is the logical suspect. Constance must have rolled Lola's body in the carpet and moved it into the hall for some reason."

"Returning to my role of devil's advocate," Jasper said, "why would Constance do that? Put the body in a rug, then move the rug to the hall, I mean. For now, let's leave aside the whole question of why Constance would turn to murder in the first place."

I slumped. "I have no idea."

"I do."

"You do? What is it?"

"South Regent Mansions has a daily maid service, correct?"

"Yes, it's one of the selling points—a full-service flat." I felt my eyes widen as I realized the implication. "Oh, I see. Of course. The maid arrives midday."

Jasper nodded. "Right. If your suppositions are correct about Constance, she wouldn't want to tell the maid to skip her flat that day. Much better to let the maid do her job. If any questions arose later, then the maid could state she'd been in the flat, and there had been no dead body there."

I straightened as I worked it out. "So, Constance rolled the body in the rug, dragged it to the hall, and propped it up against the doorframe of the Kemps' flat. Anyone seeing it would assume it was part of the household goods that were being moved that day."

"Do you think Constance has the strength to do that?" Jasper asked. "A body is quite a heavy thing to move. And before you ask, I speak from experience . . . that of propelling heavily inebriated companions home after a party or a late night at the club. It's hard enough to drag them home when they're barely conscious."

"Constance is a sturdy young woman. It's not beyond the bounds of believability that she could drag a rug outside her flat. And no one would give it a second look. One would glance at it and move on, exactly as I did. Only someone descending in a lift would get a glimpse of a blue foot when they were perfectly on eye level with the bottom of the rug."

"How long does the maid spend in each flat?" Jasper asked.

"Usually a quarter of an hour. The maid arrives here at a quarter after twelve and leaves at half past."

"A relatively small window of time."

"Yes, but I know that on Monday the maid finished here at half-past twelve because I followed her out. She went next door to Constance and Lola's flat. I saw her go in. As I left, I noticed the rug was propped up on the Kemps' door-frame. Minerva didn't leave until twelve forty-four, and by the time she'd traveled down to the lobby and returned, it would have been after twelve forty-five. The maid would have moved on to the next flat by then. It would only take a few seconds for Constance to drag the rug back inside her flat and close the door so that when Minerva came back up in the lift, the rug was gone. That makes perfect sense. You're pretty brainy yourself," I said to Jasper.

He inclined his head. "Thank you. Happy to be of service." He picked up the teapot. "Another cup?" I shook my head as he said, "I do have one quibble, though."

"Back to being an advocate for the darker side, I see. Removing the rug for the arrival of the maid was your idea, remember."

"It's nothing to do with that. It's something else entirely." Jasper poured tea into his cup and added a sugar cube. "Didn't you say you saw Lola on Monday evening before your dinner with Minerva?"

I closed my eyes briefly. "It upsets me terribly when I think about it now, to realize I was so easily taken in. I *thought* I saw Lola, but it was Constance."

Jasper stopped stirring his tea. "Constance? Are you sure?"

"As sure as I can be. From the moment I saw the letter from Lola's mother in the handbag, I've been going over everything that's happened. Now I see that I made assumptions. My perception of what I saw and what was really there were two different things. I was wrong—*so* incredibly wrong."

"How so?"

"I thought I saw Lola, but in fact, what I saw was a woman wearing her mint-green coat and hat. I *assumed* it was Lola, but I never actually got a good look at her face. It was dark and raining, and the umbrella Evans held over her obscured my view."

"But it could have been Lola."

"No. Now that I think about it, I remember the way the woman walked. She stamped through the puddles with a heavy tread. Lola didn't move that way. She was more— well, delicate in her steps—that's the only way I can describe it."

Jasper looked doubtful, so I went on. "If you live next door to someone, you associate certain sounds with certain neighbors. Miss Bobbin brings to mind a high-pitched yip because of Ace. Mr. Popinjay is always associated with the quiet patter of cat's paws—usually followed by yipping and hissing because Miss Bobbin's dog chases his cat up and down the hall so frequently. Mrs. Attenborough has a stately tread as if she's presenting at Court. I heard Lola and Constance moving next door all the time. Lola had a light tread, like a dancer. Constance's stride is heavier. More of a trudge, really. And the woman moving to the taxi that day stomped." My insides twisted at the thought that Lola was already dead when I spoke to Constance downstairs in the drizzle. "Constance was careful, too, not to turn around and let me see her. The cloche hid her face, and the swoop of the feather over her cheek helped as well, but she never turned fully back to face me when I spoke to her."

Jasper stood and retrieved my saucer and teacup from the windowsill. "You need more tea."

"I think I do."

As the steamy liquid bubbled into my cup, Jasper said, "So you believe Constance dressed in Lola's distinctive coat and hat and carried her handbag that evening?"

"Yes. I believe she went out so Evans would see her. Any other residents who noticed the coat and hat would be a bonus." I took the cup Jasper handed me and made a face. "Like me. Constance also wore the coat and hat when she took the Flying Scotsman."

"Which enabled her to say that Lola had left town."

"Yes. I wonder if my request to meet with Lola prompted the trip to Scotland."

Jasper returned to his seat. "I doubt it. If your theory is correct, it has the sound of an intricate plan. Not something done on a whim, which brings up my next question."

"I think I know what it is—how did Constance . . ."

" . . . do away with Lola," Jasper said, supplying the end of the sentence. "Yes, that's what I was wondering. Wouldn't there be evidence of some sort—especially if the maid arrived to clean? Did you see anything that would indicate someone had died there?"

"No, but if Constance did it while Lola was in the bath
. . ."

"Oh yes. I see what you mean. Like the brides in the bath." Although it had been nearly a decade since the sensational murder trial, I still remembered the details of the man who had drowned several women in their bath.

"And it would explain why the foot was bare."

"Yes," Jasper said. "Then there's only one more question. How did Constance get the body out of the flat?"

"That I still don't know. According to Evans, no one uses the basement but Underhill. And even though Evans helps Underhill arrive and depart secretly through the basement, I do think he'd draw the line at removing a dead body."

"You're probably right. It's a rather large favor to ask." We both sat in silence for a moment, then Jasper said, "I don't suppose you noticed any luggage missing in flat 225?"

"No. Constance's room was in such a state that it was difficult to see anything besides the mess. And I didn't even think to look in Lola's closet. I wish I had."

"I definitely advise against returning to that flat," Jasper said quickly.

"No. I don't want to do that. Besides, their trunks might be stored in the attic. That's where mine are."

Silence enveloped us again, then I sat forward. "If their trunks are in the attic, Evans would know. He'll have records."

"Yes," Jasper said. "Why don't we ask Evans?"

CHAPTER TWENTY-THREE

*T*he lift stopped with its usual bounce on the ground floor, and Jasper slid back the metal gate. The lobby was empty at the moment, and I led the way to the alcove where Evans was sorting papers on his counter.

When he saw me, his expression became guarded. "Hello, Miss Belgrave. How can I help you?"

"Hello again, Evans. Don't worry, I'm not here to continue our prior conversation."

"Then what can I do for you?" He sounded relieved.

"It's a simple thing. Did anyone from flat 225 request something be brought down from the attic recently?"

I expected him to go to his ledger, but he didn't make a move to look anything up. He said immediately, "Yes, Miss Mallory rang up and asked me to bring down her large trunk."

"Did that happen earlier in the week?"

"Yes, on Monday."

Jasper and I exchanged a look, then Jasper propped his

elbow on the counter and tapped the ledger. "You have an impressive memory. You didn't even have to check your notes."

"It was a memorable trunk. Hefty."

"Oh?" Jasper said. "Large, was it?"

Evans' hand hovered at his thigh to indicate the size. "Nicely made too. Reinforced leather edges and brass hardware. Very nice. Practically a steamer trunk." His eyebrows descended as he frowned. "Miss Belgrave, are you all right? You look sickly."

I drew in a deep breath and made an effort to appear as if this was a normal conversation. "Yes. Fine, thank you. Did you deliver the trunk to flat 225 yourself?"

"That's right. Miss Mallory had me leave it inside the front door."

Jasper said, "Rather unusual, that. One would think that with something as unwieldy as a trunk that size, a lady would want it taken to one of the bedrooms."

"Miss Mallory was preparing to go out. She was putting on her hat, in fact. She told me to leave the trunk there inside the door, and she'd see to it later."

I thought back to my quick survey of the flat and remembered a mirror hung about halfway down the hallway between the front door and the kitchen. "Let me guess. Miss Mallory was facing the mirror, adjusting her cloche, which was a light green color and matched her coat."

Evans stared at me a moment. "You *are* quite the detective lady, Miss Belgrave. That's exactly what she was wearing."

Normally I'd be pleased to have worked out the small

details, but I couldn't draw much satisfaction from what I was learning, not when it confirmed such a grim supposition. "And she spoke to you over her shoulder?"

"Yes. It happened just like that."

"You never spoke to her face-to-face?" Jasper asked.

"No. I wished her good day and left."

Jasper's face shifted into a rather grim expression, and I knew his thoughts were tracking along the same dark pathway mine were. I turned back to Evans. "And did you bring the trunk down for Miss Mallory later?"

"Yes, but it wasn't that day." He turned a few pages back in the ledger, then ran his thick finger down a column. He tapped a line. "Yes. Tuesday morning. She wanted a taxi. I brought the trunk down and loaded it. She was on her way to King's Cross."

"What was it like when you brought it down?" I asked.

"What do you mean?"

"Was it light? Heavy?"

"Heavy enough that I asked her if she was sailing for America," Evans spoke slowly, smoothing down his walrus-like mustache. "Bit of a joke, you know," he said, his gaze bobbing between Jasper and me, his expression growing more concerned by the moment. "But she said no, she was going to Edinburgh."

"And did you get a good look at her face on Tuesday?" I asked.

"No, when I went up to get the trunk, she said she'd be right behind me and sent me down with it to get a taxi. When she came out of the building, the cabbie and I were busy loading it."

"Did you speak to her again when you opened the motor's door for her?" I asked.

"No, the cabbie did that."

"So you never saw her face."

"I couldn't, could I? Not when she was sneezing and blowing her nose."

"And she kept her handkerchief to her face as she got in the taxi, I bet," I said.

"Yes, that's how it was," Evans said, but he didn't seem surprised by the accuracy of my guess. The wrinkles in his forehead deepened with each question I asked.

"And have you seen Miss Mallory since then?"

"No, she's not returned from Edinburgh." He turned the pages carefully back to the section where he was making notes on today's activities, then smoothed his large palm along the book's gutter. "This has something to do with your investigation. You think something funny was going on in the young ladies' flat?"

"I'm afraid so. But we'd best keep this among ourselves for now."

"Of course. I won't even make a note of it in the ledger. Normally, I'd jot down what we talked about in case it came up later." He tapped his forehead. "The old brain box can't hold everything, you know, but I'll skip that."

"Thank you for your discretion." I tucked a few notes under the blotter.

"There's no need for that, Miss Belgrave." Evans slid the folded money out from under the heavy book and reached out to return it, but I took a step back.

"Consider it a thank you for putting up with my nosy questions," I said.

His thick mustache shifted as he smiled. "I'm always happy to help the residents. It's my job."

"Then consider that a bonus." I took a few steps toward the lift, when his words about the ledger sparked an idea. I hurried back and gripped the counter. "Evans, you note down everything that happens?"

"Yes. When people come and go, deliveries, visitors, everything."

"Even the arrival of telegrams?"

"Oh yes. Some residents want to know exactly when a package or telegram arrived."

"Excellent. On Monday, did a telegram arrive for Miss Mallory?"

Evans' thick eyebrows descended again. "I don't believe so." He turned the pages back and ran his fingers down the columns again. He went through the motion twice, then looked up and shook his head. "No. No telegram arrived for flat 225 on Monday."

"Evans, you've been quite helpful. That's just what I needed to know. And please, not a word about the trunk or telegram to anyone yet."

"I don't seem to remember anything about a trunk or telegram," he said, his expression taking on a vacant look.

"Thank you, Evans."

"Happy to help. If there's something funny going on, I want it stopped. This is a nice place to work, and I want to keep my position."

"Oh, I think you—and your ledger—will be invaluable in sorting this out."

As Jasper and I returned to the lift, I said in a low voice, "We're on the right track. I suppose it's wrong of me to feel a tiny surge of elation, but I do."

"Despite the circumstances, discovering the truth is satisfying," Jasper said.

"Of course, it's rather dampened by the knowledge that the lies we've uncovered mean it looks more certain than ever that Constance murdered Lola."

Movement of the lobby doors drew my attention, and I was surprised to see Minerva nodding to the doorman as she came inside.

I crossed the lobby to her. "Minerva, I didn't expect you back so soon. How is your mother?"

"Fine. Unexpectedly fine. She doesn't need me at all, in fact." She greeted Jasper, then turned back to me. "The situation is not at all what I thought. Mother's arm is sprained, not broken. There was some mangling of the message from the doctor. A few weeks of rest, and she'll be back to normal."

"Oh, I'm so glad to hear it."

"And the vicar's wife has a sister, a widow, who is visiting the parish. She'd like to stay on in the village. My mother has arranged with her—the widowed sister—to move in and take care of the cooking and cleaning. Apparently the woman's at a bit of a loose end. Her only daughter recently married and departed for Canada with her new husband. Both my mother and the widowed sister are delighted with the arrangement. All my worries about her were quite unfounded. The village doctor assured me her moments of forgetfulness are typical for her age and nothing to worry about. And my mother informed me in quite a bossy way that she is quite capable of arranging things in her life. She told me to return to London and come back for a visit in a few weeks."

"That is good news."

"Yes, it's worked out rather well. Has anything happened while I was gone?"

I drew her toward the lift. "So much."

CHAPTER TWENTY-FOUR

*J*asper and I accompanied Minerva upstairs to her flat. We waited in silence while the doorman dropped off her suitcase. Once Jasper closed the door behind him, Minerva asked, "What have you found out?" She hadn't removed her hat or coat, and her gloved fingers gripped her handbag strap.

I motioned to the sofa. "Let's sit down, and I'll tell you all about it."

She stepped back and waved us into the sitting room. "I've forgotten my manners. Yes, please come in."

"And perhaps Jasper could get us a drink?" I caught his glance, then shifted my gaze to the drinks cabinet in the dining room.

Minerva perched on the edge of the chair and tugged on the fingers of her gloves to work them off her hands. "As bad as that, is it?"

"It's not good news," I said as the click of glass came from the dining room. Minerva put her gloves in her bag, then linked her fingers together around her knees and waited, her posture braced.

"I'm afraid it was Lola who was wrapped up in the rug."

Minerva didn't move, but all the color washed out of her face. "Oh, that's terrible."

Jasper handed her a brandy snifter, and she took it automatically.

"Have a little. It will help with the shock."

She sipped, then drew in a deep breath. "Are you sure, Olive?"

"As sure as I can be," I said, then I told her what Jasper and I had discovered. "So, you see, it wasn't anything at all to do with the Darkwaiths' flat or anything related to the basement. Constance must have put the body into Lola's large trunk and marched out through the lobby with Evans toting it to the cab for her."

Minerva had taken a few more sips of her brandy, and now her complexion looked pale instead of dead white. "That's awful. Why would Constance do that?"

"Greed, I think. Constance has certainly proved she can fool people—at least momentarily—into thinking that she's Lola. If Constance is able to maintain the fiction that Lola is simply away, Constance will have access to everything that belonged to Lola. As long as she can produce a reasonable facsimile of Lola's signature, Constance can make withdrawals from Lola's bank."

Jasper had started a fire, and now he stood with the poker in his hand, nursing it into a blaze. "She might even move the account to another institution. It would be a bold move, but also the smartest play. She wouldn't have to deal with tellers and managers who knew Lola."

Minerva let out a ragged sigh. "I'd almost hoped I was wrong—even though that would have meant there was something wrong up here"—she tapped her temple—"but to know I was right ..." She downed the rest of the brandy in a gulp. "Well, that's a different kind of horrible. Where is the trunk now?"

The question stung. It had been bothering me, pricking at me, ever since Jasper and I learned that a woman who looked like Lola had left South Regent Mansions with a large trunk on Tuesday. "I don't know. That's the weak spot in the argument, and I know the police will zero in on it. If Constance dressed as Lola and took the Flying Scotsman as far as York but got off the train there, it would make sense that she'd have the luggage taken off the train as well."

Jasper put away the poker and leaned a shoulder on the mantel. "Yes, because if she'd left the trunk on the train, it would be discovered when all the passengers disembarked."

"So, I bet Constance changed into a different hat and coat, something more nondescript—she must have brought that with her—as soon as she arrived in York. Once she was out of the eye-catching mint-green coat and hat, she could leave the trunk in the cloakroom in York. Then she returned to London either that night or the next day in her usual clothing."

"How truly appalling," Minerva said. "That's why you found Lola's beautiful coat and hat in Constance's room." The fire popped, the only sound in the room, then Minerva drew a deep breath. "Thank you for being persistent, Olive. You fulfilled your end of the bargain. In fact, you did more than I asked. You not only discovered who is missing, but you have a location the police can look for the body. Now I'll do what I promised." She put her empty glass down on the coffee table and removed her gloves from her handbag. "Go to the police." She looked sick at the prospect as she pulled on her gloves with jerky movements.

"If I might make a suggestion," I said.

Minerva glanced up. "Please do. Especially if it involves a delay in contacting the police."

"Only a slight delay, but I think it's the best approach. Let me contact Inspector Longly. He's engaged to my cousin and—overall—he's a reasonable chap. He'll hear you out, and if we emphasize the need for discretion, I think he'll do all he can to make sure the situation is investigated as quietly as possible."

Minerva's hands fell into her lap. "Thank you, Olive. I'd appreciate that. The thought of going to a police station does sound rather ghastly."

"I'll see if he can come here. Perhaps my flat?"

"Yes, that would be good. All right, then." She stood. "I should change out of my traveling suit and order my thoughts. I must appear as competent and in my right mind as possible."

I wasn't keen on the idea of leaving Minerva alone just then, but I put her brandy snifter in the sink, and Jasper and I left her flat. As I crossed the hall, Jasper checked his wristwatch. I paused, my hand on the doorknob of my flat. "Are you staying on?"

"I hate to abandon you at this point, but I do have an appointment that I need to keep. It shouldn't take long."

"An appointment of the hush-hush variety, I imagine."

Jasper simply smiled.

"Go on with you, then," I said. "I'll let you know how it goes."

"And you really intend to drop it all in Inspector Longly's lap?"

"Yes, as much as I dislike doing so without answers to absolutely all my questions."

"But you're wise enough to know that it's time for the police to step in." He settled his fedora on his head. "I'm quite proud of you for offering to call Longly instead of continuing to pursue this on your own."

I pulled a face. "As much as I dislike contacting him, I've learned that pushing on alone can have dreadful consequences. I don't want to be in that situation again."

Inspector Longly was right on time. At his knock, Minerva's teacup clattered into her saucer. I gave her an encouraging smile before I went to answer the door.

"Hello, Inspector," I said as I ushered him into the sitting room. Longly was in his early thirties and had light brown hair and a thin mustache. I made an effort to address him by his given name, Louis, when I met him in company with my cousin Gwen, but this seemed an occasion to use his title. I'd recently seen him in relaxed social situations—dinner parties and family events—in Gwen's company, and I'd had a glimpse of his off-duty side, but today he'd reverted to his reserved detective inspector manner. I was happy to see that he was alone. Longly must have left his sergeant behind out of deference to my request to keep the interview as informal as possible.

I introduced him to Minerva. The only sign of her nervousness was her hands as they fluttered to smooth her dress as she stood. Minerva was again in her severe gray suit. With her hair pulled back in a chignon and her bright lipstick toned down, she looked as if she was ready to take dictation from a senior partner at some long-established firm.

Longly, a veteran of the Great War, had his sleeve pinned to his suit jacket, and there could have been an awkward moment when Minerva reached out automatically with her right hand to shake his hand, then halted. He lifted his right shoulder, which shifted the empty sleeve. "I usually just make do with a nod." He smoothed over the tricky moment with a smile that seemed to put Minerva at ease. "Pleased to meet you, Miss Blythe."

He accepted a cup of tea, took one sip, and set it aside. He then pulled a small notebook from his pocket, and with deft, practiced movements, he opened it one-handed and took up a pencil that had bookmarked the first blank page. "Now, Olive tells me there are some issues here at South Regent Mansions that need investigating. Why don't you tell me your address and telephone number before we get started."

He took down Minerva's information, and it was clear that he'd become quite used to writing with his left hand.

He circled around the pencil and used the side of his hand to hold the notebook in place. He took down the details as rapidly as Minerva spoke. Once the preliminaries were out of the way, he said, "So tell me about the situation."

Minerva cleared her throat. "It began on Monday. I had an appointment at Fleet Street. I looked at the clock as I went out the door because I was cutting it rather fine. It was twelve forty-four ..."

Longly let her tell it at her own pace. She went through the day chronologically, describing what she'd seen, her reaction to it, and the reason she hadn't contacted the police right away. Longly didn't comment, only nodded and wrote in his notebook.

When she reached the point of describing how she'd recruited me to investigate, his gaze flickered to me, but he didn't interrupt. Minerva described how we'd worked out that the body was probably someone who lived on the second floor. "Olive should tell you the rest, about how she checked on all the residents," Minerva said, the tension easing out of her voice as she handed the narrative off to me.

Longly shifted toward me, and I skimmed through the essentials of how I verified that each person in the building was alive and well. I kept my description brief—particularly in the case of the Darkwaiths' flat. I described how I thought I'd confirmed everyone was accounted for, then said, "But I was wrong. I'd made a mistake. I realized it when I was in Constance and Lola's flat."

I detailed what I'd found in the flat, skirting around how I'd actually gotten in. I *might* have given the impression that

Lola had given me a key because I was a neighbor. I hurried on to describe how I hadn't actually seen Lola face-to-face and how Constance had masqueraded as Lola, fooling me on Monday evening. I told him about the trunk and how Constance had continued to impersonate Lola on the Flying Scotsman as well as our suppositions that the trunk was in luggage left in the cloakroom in the train station in York.

When I finished, Longly paused as if he had so many questions that he had to decide where to begin. Finally, he turned his attention back to Minerva. "Did you see any identifying marks on the foot? Anything at all? A scratch? A freckle? Even a corn? Anything?"

"No, I didn't see anything like that, but I did draw this for you." She picked up her sketchbook from the table beside her, opened it, then turned it so he could see her drawing of the rug propped against the doorframe of the Kemps' flat.

The image had her usual economy of strokes, and her simple style only increased the impact of the chilling image.

Longly said, "May I keep this?"

"Of course." She pressed down on the opposite page to hold the sketchbook flat and tore the page from the binding.

Longly thanked her and placed it in an interior pocket of his jacket, then looked back to me. "So, the evidence you have is that Miss Dolores Mallory's handbag is in her flat along with a very expensive coat and matching hat."

"Yes, and the fact that the handbag contained a precious letter that Lola told me she always kept with her."

Longly nodded, but I could see that he wasn't convinced. "It's a rather fragile base for an accusation."

I scooted forward on my chair. "Then where's Lola? There's no trace of her here at South Regent Mansions. Evans hasn't seen her since Monday—and I'm *sure* that it wasn't Lola that Evans saw. It was Constance wearing Lola's coat and hat. Constance has been avoiding me. I've asked her several times for an address and tried to find out where Lola is in Edinburgh, and each time Constance puts me off. Lola's disappeared. That's the most compelling piece of evidence. It's not fragile at all. I'm sure you'll find all the evidence you need in the left luggage in York station's cloakroom."

Someone rapped on my door, and I frowned. I wasn't expecting anyone, unless Jasper had returned, but he usually rang up before arriving. "Excuse me," I said, and Minerva sent me a brief, pleading look. I knew she didn't want to be left alone with Longly, so I excused myself and paced quickly out of the sitting room. Longly asked Minerva another question about what she'd done the afternoon immediately after she'd seen the rolled carpet.

I'd dispatch whoever was in the hall and get back to the sitting room as soon as possible, but when I flung the door open, Constance stood on the other side of the threshold. "I only have a moment." She held a piece of paper out. "I finally have Lola's address in Edinburgh."

I was so stunned that I didn't move for a moment.

Constance flapped the paper. "Well, do you want it or not?"

"Yes, of course." I took the paper. "You've heard from Lola? Did you speak to her?"

The chime on the lift rang out as it arrived. Constance

glanced over her shoulder at it, then looked back at me. "I'm sorry. I must run or I'll be late for work, but I did want to hand that address off to you. You've been so insistent on getting in touch with her." She spoke the last few words as she walked backward, then turned and hurried for the lift. She whipped back the gate and dodged inside, sliding the metal slats closed as the lift descended.

I raced back to the sitting room and interrupted Minerva's soft tones. "I don't believe it. Constance just brought me Lola's address in Edinburgh." I held up the paper.

Longly stood, and I said, "If you hurry, you can still catch her."

"It's better if I don't approach her at this point." He slipped his notebook into his pocket. "May I see the note?"

"Of course." The paper was a single sheet, folded in half. He gripped it by the edge and angled it so it fell open, tilting his head to read the address. "Central Edinburgh, if I'm not mistaken. I'll have a colleague check this for me."

He put it away in his suit coat pocket, then moved around to the table where I'd placed his hat. He nodded to both of us and said, "Thank you for the information you shared with me today, and for your drawing, Miss Blythe. I'll look into everything and let you know what I find out."

CHAPTER TWENTY-FIVE

"Unbelievable!" I dropped down onto the sofa. "For Constance to finally produce Lola's address now! I don't believe it. I just don't."

Minerva said, "As much as I'd like Lola to be alive—even though that would mean I was mistaken about what I saw—I don't believe it either. Constance is lying. It's as simple as that. Once the inspector checks on it, he'll realize that too."

"What's brought about this sudden change in your attitude about the police? Why the sudden faith in them?"

"Inspector Longly wasn't at all what I expected. He actually listened to me, and I feel"—she tilted her head and considered the empty fireplace—"relieved. Yes, that's it. Relieved to have handed the whole thing off to the inspector. I believe he'll look into everything, just as he said. If he does that . . . well, we know what he'll find. Lola truly is missing, and once he checks the cloakroom in York . . ." She trailed off and crossed her arms as if she were cold. "You shouldn't be so upset. Constance providing the address will

219

prove your point to the inspector better than any argument we could make."

"Yes, that's true," I allowed.

Minerva began to gather the empty cups and put them on the tea tray. "The only thing to do now is wait."

"I hate waiting."

"I know you do, Olive. You'd much rather dash up to York and Edinburgh. You might as well let the inspector do his job. It would take you hours and hours just to get to York, not to mention Edinburgh. Inspector Longly will probably have an answer before the night is out. In fact, I bet he's back here in a few hours knocking on Constance's door."

"I also hate it when your logic is irrefutable."

Minerva smiled as she pushed herself to her feet. "Well, *I* hate to leave, but I must dress for the birthday party at Rules. At least it will take my mind off things for a bit."

"The party at Rules?" I asked.

"Old Harrison's birthday, remember?"

"That's tonight? I didn't realize. You're going?"

"Now that I'm back in town, I have no excuse not to go. If he finds out I'm back in London and didn't attend, he'll see it as a snub. It will only give him more ammunition to add to his usual slights and digs, and it will solidify his efforts to get me removed."

After Minerva left, I did the washing up, then went for a long walk through the neighborhood in the twilight, thinking that the physical movement might reduce my itchy and restless state. I returned to South Regent Mansions tired and with my cheeks chilled from the wintry air, but impatience still simmered through me.

I rolled a fresh sheet of paper into the Remington and banged my way through several pages of touch-typing practice lessons. The activity would at least get my mind off of things. I was on my third exercise when a tap on the door interrupted me.

Minerva was pulling on her evening cloak, and I had a glimpse of her sapphire velvet gown dotted with crystal beads before she fastened the buttons on her cloak. Normally, I would have commented on how nice she looked, but one glance at her dejected face drove all thoughts of fashion out of my mind. "You've heard from Inspector Longly?"

"He telephoned. There's no suspicious unclaimed trunk in the left luggage at the train station in York."

I was so gobsmacked that it took me a moment to find a single word. "What?"

She nodded, her face miserable. "I know, but that's what he said. And it gets worse. His colleague went to the address in Edinburgh, posing as a collector for a veteran's charity. Lola was there."

"But that *can't* be right."

"Exactly what I thought. I quizzed him on it, but he was adamant."

"But then why was there such a delay in sending her address?" I asked. "Why has it been so difficult to contact her?"

"Apparently her relative was gravely ill. Sending

messages—or returning Constance's messages—was the last thing on Lola's mind."

"He's *sure* it's Lola?"

"Yes. Blonde hair, fair skin, and a pert nose," Minerva said.

"That was the description from the police? Sounds as if Longly's colleague was rather smitten."

My words brought a small smile to Minerva's face. "No. The inspector asked that they check the newspaper morgue for a picture before going to the address. The inspector's colleague reported that the woman looked like the photographs of Lola that were taken at her grandfather's funeral. So, the case is closed."

"Closed?" My voice rose above its usual pitch. "On the evidence of one woman's statement and an old newspaper photo? Did Inspector Longly actually *say* the case was closed?"

"As good as. He was polite, but I got the sense that he had more pressing matters to deal with."

"That's dismaying," I said. *And not at all like Longly,* I thought, but I kept that to myself. Perhaps there was more to Longly's investigation than Minerva realized. Longly wouldn't share all the details of a case with a witness—I knew that from personal experience. In any event, he didn't usually take the easy way out. "I wonder how recent the photograph was."

Minerva fiddled with the clasp on her clutch handbag. "The same thought occurred to me. Those pictures are awfully grainy." She blew out a deep sigh. "I was so sure you were right about what happened. I doubted myself about what I saw that first day, but now I'm *quite* sure I was right."

"I think you were too."

"But if the police won't pursue it, what is there to do?"

"Let's not give up yet. Perhaps this woman in Edinburgh is an imposter."

"You think so?" She jumped on my suggestion with an eagerness that indicated she'd considered the idea as well. "I confess, the same thought occurred to me—that Constance arranged for someone who looked like Lola to be at the address. But that's rather a lot of trouble to go to, isn't it?"

"Think of the money, though. There's a fortune at stake. If I kept pushing and continuing to try to reach Lola, it would eventually raise questions—awkward questions for Constance. What better way to resolve my questions than to give me an address and have someone there to receive anything I send? Perhaps Constance was afraid I'd hand-deliver my report. I tried to do that earlier this week. I'm sure one could find an actress to play the part of the young woman for a few days."

The carriage clock inside my flat struck the quarter hour, and Minerva's mouth turned down in a grimace. "I'm not in the mood for a party, but I should go."

"Yes, go. If the company isn't to your taste, at least the food will be excellent. I'll see if I can wheedle some more information out of Longly."

"You think you'll be able to do that?"

"I'm certainly going to try."

Minerva left, and I rang up Longly's office, but I was only able to leave a message. I returned the receiver to the cradle and tapped my fingers on the desk. Perhaps I should ring Gwen? She'd have Longly's home number. I debated it, but in the end, I pushed the telephone to the back corner of the desk and returned to finish my typing exercise.

I tended to forge ahead when I got an idea, but I was learning that moving headlong into action sometimes brought about unexpected repercussions. I didn't want Inspector Longly to think I was going behind his back and trying to manipulate him through Gwen. And I certainly didn't want to cause a quarrel between Gwen and Longly. Although if he had closed the case, I wasn't beyond tugging on a string, if that was a last resort. I would be patient and wait for Longly to return my message. I knew he would. Constance wasn't aware we'd pointed the police in her direction. I'd give him an hour, and if I didn't hear from him by then, I'd contact Gwen. I rang up Jasper instead to share what had happened, but Grigsby informed me, his voice dripping with disapproval—he believed young ladies should not telephone gentlemen—that Jasper was out as well.

I seemed to be the only person at home. I threw myself into my desk chair and finished my touch-typing exercises. But they were truly poor specimens filled with mistakes because the questions simmering through the back of my mind refused to fade away. I stretched my hands out in front of me to relax my shoulders, then I drew the curtains against the evening darkness. The night was studded with dots of streetlights and flat windows that glowed against the black background like the crystal beads on Minerva's velvet dress. Restless, I checked the clock—only half an hour gone —and paced around the flat. Finally, I turned on the radio, and the strains of a jazz orchestra filled the flat. Then I rang up the service kitchen and ordered a dinner of soup, rolls, and cheese.

I was toasting the rolls in the kitchen, thinking my dinner was quite a contrast from the roast saddle of mutton that Minerva was probably having, when the shrill ring of the telephone overpowered the music from the radio. I dashed for the telephone, expecting Longly's voice, but the instant I answered, Minerva's staccato voice cut over my greeting, her words infused with excitement. "Olive, Constance is here."

"She's at Rules this evening as well?"

"Yes, her dinner companion has black hair combed back from his forehead, a narrow mustache, and an extremely self-satisfied manner. If I were drawing him, I'd put a smirk on his full lips."

It sounded like the man I'd seen with her outside the theater, who I thought was Alec Woodwiss, but before I could say that, Minerva rushed on with her monologue. "I've done something rather reckless. I was watching them, laughing and enjoying themselves, and thinking of poor Lola. It's so terribly *wrong*, Olive, what with the police washing their hands of it."

"I know—"

I managed to edge the two words in, but Minerva barely paused before she said, "So I decided to do something. I stepped away from the table. I went to the lobby—that's where I'm ringing you from, the lobby telephone—where I requested paper and pencil. I wrote a note and tipped the maître d' to have it delivered to Constance's table."

"Didn't they see you?"

"Those two? No, they're completely wrapped up in themselves. I went back to my table and positioned my chair so that they wouldn't see me if they looked across the room, but I could see them. The man at the table across from me has a rather wide girth and blocked me from their view, but if I leaned a little to the side, I had a perfectly clear view of Constance's face. When she opened the note and read it, Constance went as white as the tablecloth and dropped the note as if it had burned her fingers. She immediately turned to the man with her. I could hear the panicked tone of her voice from several tables away."

I wanted to scold Minerva for taking such a risk—after all, she'd counseled me to be patient earlier this evening—but my curiosity won out. "What did she say?"

"I couldn't make out the words, only that she was frantic. The man was making placating sounds and glancing around the room, trying to calm her down."

"Goodness. What did your note say?"

"I know where you put Lola's body."

CHAPTER TWENTY-SIX

"Goodness, Minerva!" I said. "But we don't know where Lola's body is! I can't believe you did that."

"There's a time to be bold and a time to lie low. This was a time to be bold." Now that Minerva had gotten the gist of her story out, her words coming through the telephone line had slowed. "It seemed to be the perfect chance to find out if we were right. I believe, from Constance's reaction, that we are."

"I can't argue with you there," I said.

"I slipped away from dinner again to ring you because Constance and the man are clearing out. They called for their bill."

"You *have* rattled them."

"Yes," she said, her voice infused with satisfaction, then her tone turned businesslike. "I walked behind their table just now, and I managed to catch a couple of scraps of their conversation. The man is bringing Constance back to South Regent Mansions. Lola's motor is in the courtyard, and they're going to take it to check on where they ..." Minerva swallowed, then it seemed she had to force out her next words, " . . . left her. Lola, I mean. They mentioned somewhere called Ashwick—at least, I think that's what they said."

"Never heard of it."

"Me either. I don't know if it's a town or village or an estate . . . but I think that's where they're going."

"Then we need to get in touch with Inspector Longly immediately," I said.

"I tried ringing him before you and had to leave a message. Who knows when he'll get my message? Maybe not until tomorrow morning. I'll make my excuses and come back to the flat. I'm suddenly feeling very ill."

"I think it would be better if you stayed there. If they catch sight of you now, they might suspect the note came from you. After all, you live on the second floor of South Regent Mansions. You're probably the only person in the restaurant who knows them and also knew Lola."

"But they haven't seen me."

"You don't *think* they have, but what about that enormous mirror in the dining room of Rules? They might have seen your reflection and already suspect you sent the note. I think you're in an extremely dangerous position. Taking a taxi and traveling through London alone is not a good idea. You said you're in the restaurant's entry?"

"Yes. I can see into the dining room, and I've been watching it the whole time we've talked. They haven't left yet."

"Then you stay put. Let them leave, then return to your

party. I'll telephone Inspector Longly and tell him what's happened."

"But he's not in."

"I have another way to reach him."

A little later, I stood behind the trunk of a chestnut tree in the park across the street from South Regent Mansions, my breath making little white puffs. It wasn't long before a taxi arrived and a couple climbed out. I wasn't able to see the man's face, but I recognized Constance as she emerged from the back seat in a swirl of her evening cloak. The man paused for her to walk ahead of him, and she stamped up the steps and into the building. I set off, walking confidently as if I took a moonlit stroll around London every evening. I circled around the building and took up a position in the doorway alcove of a shop where I had a view of the entrance to the courtyard at the back of South Regent Mansions.

I'd employed all possible ways to reach Longly, but I hadn't been successful. I'd left another message for him at his office, then I'd rung up Gwen at Parkview Hall, but she was also out. She, along with the rest of the family, were dining with neighbors who weren't on the telephone. Brimble, Parkview's butler, didn't have Inspector Longly's home telephone number. "I'm afraid the need to contact the young man at his residence has never arisen, Miss Olive," he'd said, his tone deeply regretful. "I will tell Miss Gwen you telephoned the moment she arrives home."

"Thank you, Brimble," I'd said. But by then it would be too late. "There's no need to worry her. I'll ring up tomorrow and speak to her."

"Very good, miss."

A second attempt to breach the defenses of the police's desk sergeant and convince him to give me Longly's home telephone number had also failed, so I'd changed into jodhpurs and put on my sturdiest shoes. I'd pulled on my thick wool coat along with my hat and gloves. Since I couldn't alert Longly and let him know that he needed to follow Constance, I'd do it myself.

I'd been patient. I'd attempted to go through the proper channels. But that hadn't worked, so I was moving forward. I felt like one of the wind-up toys I'd played with as a child that zipped around once the spring was released. It was a relief to take action—even if it was only standing in the dark watching for Constance's return.

A spattering of rain had fallen earlier, but now the sky was cloudless. The puddles left after the spurt of rain were now icy and reflected back the streetlights like a mirror. A frigid breeze teased at my ears and the back of my neck. I pulled my scarf up higher and wrapped my arms more tightly around the bundle I held pressed to my chest. If Constance and her companion didn't appear soon, I'd have to move around and pace to another doorway simply to keep warm.

The sound of an engine laboring along the street announced the arrival of a motor long before it turned the corner. An elderly Austin 10-hp coasted to a stop, but the engine continued to thump and rattle.

My chariot had arrived. I disengaged myself from the recess of the doorway.

Jasper stepped out and squinted in my direction. "That is you, isn't it, Olive?" He'd changed out of the suit that had the basement's grime on the sleeves. Despite the late hour, he was as immaculately turned out as ever in evening dress and a heavy wool coat.

"It is."

He opened the passenger door for me, then sprinted back to the driver's side. I scrambled into the motor, glad to be out of the direct wind, although Jasper's motor was far from airtight. Even after both doors were closed, a chilly draft whistled in through the gap between the canvas top and the windows. But I was so glad Jasper had arrived before Constance left South Regent Mansions that I didn't mind the glacial surges of air.

Jasper, rubbing his gloved hands together, nodded to the large book I placed on the seat between us. "Brought along some reading material, I see. That will help pass the time."

I removed a torch from my pocket, along with a thermos. I unscrewed the lid, and the aroma of coffee filled the motor. "A few essentials. Thank you for bringing your motor."

"All part of my Watson duties."

When I'd said goodbye to Minerva, I knew I didn't have time to get in touch with the garage where my Morris Cowley was kept, much less have it brought around. But Jasper's lodgings had a mews where he stored his motor. His Austin 10-hp was rather dilapidated compared to the modern lines of my Morris, but when one is in a pinch, one uses what is at hand. I poured some coffee in the thermos lid and handed it to him.

"You're a good egg, Olive."

"Well, a girl can't ask a man to drive her around the country in the middle of the night without offering some sort of refreshment."

"You're as thoughtful as you are demanding. Have you brought any sandwiches, by chance?"

"No time for that."

"Pity. I was hoping for something with the crusts cut off, don't you know. Now, what are we watching for? Should I shut off the engine?"

"How easy is it to start it?"

"It's rather a process—a long one."

"Then, no. Let's not do that. We're waiting for Lola's motor to depart from the back courtyard of South Regent Mansions."

"What kind of motor?"

"I'm not sure."

"Indeed? A rather scattershot approach to take."

"Yes, well, I'm working on rather sketchy details. We'll have to be close enough to see the occupants. Fortunately, it's not an incredibly busy time of the evening."

"No. London town is rather sleepy now. So what caused you to rouse me from my fireside this evening? Something significant has happened, I take it?"

"Many things have happened, but you don't look as if you were relaxing at home."

"I went around to the club for dinner after you called earlier this evening."

We'd spoken after Longly's visit, but now I brought him up to date, telling him about how the police hadn't found a suspicious abandoned trunk in York, the woman in Edinburgh who claimed to be Lola, as well as Minerva's impulsive decision to send the note to Constance at Rules.

"My," Jasper said. "Rather gutsy of her."

"I know. But it worked. Minerva provoked a reaction—a guilty reaction. I convinced Minerva to stay at the restaurant in case they'd spotted her. She overheard a snippet of their conversation. It sounded as if they're off to make sure nothing's been discovered with Lola's body—such an unpleasant thought, but exactly what we expected. Constance and the man have returned here to pick up Lola's motor. They're on their way to somewhere called Ashwick."

Jasper put the lid back on the thermos. "Don't know where that is."

"I don't either." I picked up the large book. "Thus, the atlas." I opened it to the index. "You don't mind keeping an eye out for someone departing the courtyard, do you?"

"Not at all, old bean. You peruse the cartography over there. I'll keep watch."

I shielded the light from the torch with my hand as I switched it on, but the white pages were still blindingly bright.

"Very handy to have an atlas on hand," Jasper commented, his attention focused through the windscreen.

I ran my finger down the column of place names. "It's a very important thing to have on hand. I've needed to consult an atlas a couple of times in the past. If a library or book shop isn't open, it does put one in rather a bad spot to be without one. I decided I should have my own atlas for just such a case as this."

"Excellent idea. You know I set great store by a well-stocked library."

I reached the end of the relevant column. "How odd. There's no Ashwick listed."

"Hmm, Ashwick . . ." Jasper tapped the steering wheel, his face thoughtful. "Can't say I've ever come across that name. Now, if it was *Astwick*, I *am* familiar with it. Could Minerva have been mistaken?"

"It's possible. She said she only overheard a scrap of the conversation." I checked the list again. "Yes, here it is. Astwick, and since that's the only remotely similar name, that must be it. It's listed as a manor house."

"It was a manor house. Now it's a ruin."

"Is it?"

"Yes. It caught fire in oh-eight or oh-nine. Half of it burned, and the insurance wasn't paid up. The family couldn't rebuild. They sold off what could be salvaged and moved to a terraced flat in London."

I'd turned to the appropriate map page and had located the ruined manor house. "It's not far. A little north of London proper."

"It would be a perfect place to dispose of the body."

I looked up. "You're familiar with it?"

"One of my school chums lived nearby. I visited him on one of the school holidays. My friend and I spent most of the holiday daring each other to go through the gates and explore the house. Great tumbled-down place. It provided uncommonly good fodder for ghost stories."

"I imagine it did."

"Well, if that's where we're going, then this drive could be quite long."

I switched off the torch and gathered my coat collar closer against the drafts that were wafting through the motor. "Of course, all this is speculation. If they don't actually go anywhere, then—"

"I believe . . ." Jasper stretched and peered through the windshield. "There is movement in the courtyard."

His height gave him a better view. He reached inside his coat pocket, pulled out his spectacles, and settled them on his nose. "Yes, definite movement." A pair of headlamps came on, their golden beams illuminating the bricks of the courtyard. "It looks as if we're going on a jaunt after all."

"Can you see them?" I asked. "Is it a blonde woman and a man with dark hair combed straight back?"

"Could be. Dash it! My vision isn't the best, you know." He opened his door. "Quickly, Olive, let's switch places. Your eyesight is much better than mine. If it does come to a run in the countryside, you'll be able to keep them in view better than I will."

As I scrambled out and swung into the driver's seat, the solid thuds of doors closing reverberated through the night air, then an engine purred. I slipped into the driver's seat and slunk low. Jasper joined me in ducking below the dash as the motor emerged from the courtyard. The twin beams of the headlights swung across the street, flashing across the windscreen.

I risked a peek. A pearl-gray Hispano-Suiza was moving away at a rapid pace.

Jasper picked up the atlas and found the page for central London. "You follow at a distance, and I'll try to work out if we're going toward Astwick or somewhere else. Tally-ho, old bean."

I let out the clutch. "Tally-ho, indeed."

CHAPTER TWENTY-SEVEN

*I*t was fairly easy to travel along in the wake of the Hispano-Suiza in London. There was still a little traffic about, even though it was late in the evening. Once we left the city, I dropped back as far as I dared, tooling along dark country lanes. Keeping the double pinpricks of the red taillights in sight, I followed the motor, its pearl-gray finish skimming along the ribbon of the road that threaded in and out of thick bands of trees.

The terrain became more densely wooded and hilly. I had the wheel in a death grip, and my neck muscles were tight from hunching forward to peer through the windscreen. The twin crimson dots turned off the main road, and Jasper, his head bent over the atlas with his finger tracing our route, declared, "I don't see where else they could be heading *except* Astwick."

The Hispano-Suiza turned again, and when I followed a few moments later, the Austin's headlamps briefly spotlighted a signpost for Astwick village. "Looks like you're right." As I slowed to navigate through the sleeping village, I loosened my grip and flexed my fingers, pushing my palms against the steering wheel.

Jasper closed the atlas and adjusted his spectacles as we crawled by a butcher, a greengrocer, and a church. "It's not much different from when I was here as a boy, except, of course, for the cenotaph on the green."

Once we were past the last cottage, I changed gears and pressed down on the accelerator. "How far is Astwick Manor?" The Hispano-Suiza had climbed the hill ahead of us and disappeared from sight as it descended on the other side.

"Not far. Just beyond the rise. The gate is on the right-hand side of the road, probably about two miles ahead."

"Good. It's difficult to keep them in sight with the trees and hills." We crested the rise, and the road curved away, a thin silver strip through the dark clusters of trees. In the distance, the pale gray of the Hispano-Suiza turned off the road. It bounced over rough ground, then disappeared between two stone gateposts set in a stone wall. The glow from the motor's headlamps lit up the bare tree branches beyond the crumbling walls, making it easy to trace the motor's progress.

"No gates?" I asked.

"They were sold off, like almost everything that was salvageable."

As we swooped down the hill, I said, "I don't know about you, but I don't feel too confident about taking your motor along that lane."

"I agree, it looks rough. I'm sure nothing's been done to maintain the roads."

"Right, then. We'll leave it here." We coasted to a stop on the berm of the road several yards short of the gateposts. I nudged the bonnet of the motor behind a clump of what looked like Leyland cypress, and their evergreen branches blocked the motor from view.

"There's no need for us to go in after them," Jasper said. "In fact, let's head back to London now, old bean. We now know Astwick Manor is the place to send the police to look for poor Lola's body. All you need to do is inform Longly. He'll have the place searched tomorrow."

I eyed the height of the now crumbling stone wall as well as the imposing gate posts. "Astwick Manor is sizable?"

Jasper hesitated a moment. "It is."

I fastened the top button on my coat and slipped the torch into my pocket. "And the grounds? They're extensive grounds too, I imagine."

Jasper sighed. "Yes. A parkland with a lake and an ornamental island with a folly."

"Of course. What's an estate without a lake, an island, and a folly?" I reached for the door handle. "We need to at least see where they go. Otherwise, Longly could search in there for months and not find a thing." I opened the door and stepped out. A cold wind whipped my hair across my eyes. I tucked it behind my ears, then settled my hat more securely on my head.

We both closed our doors quietly. Jasper whispered over the top of the motor, "I knew you'd take that approach, but I had to throw out the counterargument."

"Of course. I'm just glad you didn't do the gentlemanly thing and insist that I wait in the motor while you went and explored."

"Heaven forbid. I know you too well, Olive. That would never do." He extended his hand as we met in front of the motor. "Shall we?"

"Yes, let's."

We passed between the gate posts. A carpet-like moss coated the stone eagles that topped the posts, while a pale lichen filigreed the pillars. What had once been a wide avenue was now filled with undergrowth and long grass.

We passed the dilapidated gatehouse. I hadn't switched on the torch. The night was clear, and a fat moon cast a milky light that highlighted the tracks of the motor, which had crushed the vegetation.

With each of us walking along the flattened path of the tires, we moved quickly. Thick woodland extended out from each side of the lane. The trees were too dense to see where the gray motor had gone, but when the wind died down for a moment, the hum of the engine carried through the air.

Jasper, keeping his voice low, said, "The manor house is straight ahead. It's too dark to see it now, but it's at the end of this avenue." The wind whistled through the bare tree limbs above. In the undergrowth, branches shifted, indicating some nocturnal creature was on the move. We didn't speak again until we came out at the end of the avenue into what had once been a gravel clearing with a fountain. Saplings filled the space right up to the front steps of the burnt-out Italian Renaissance style mansion. It was an empty shell of broken windows and sagging rooflines. The moonlight traced along the scarred exterior where the fire had blackened the stonework.

The progress of the motor had been only slightly faster than our walk down the avenue. Tire tracks arcing through gravel indicated the Hispano-Suiza had come this way and pushed through the saplings. Then it turned off the gravel at a gap in the trees where another smaller lane cut through the woods. We stayed off the gravel and kept to the spongy undergrowth that muffled our footsteps. "If I remember correctly," Jasper said, "this lane leads to the lake."

Two flattened tracks striped the smaller lane. The motor's engine revved. "We're getting closer," I said. "They're not making much quicker progress than we are."

Jasper stepped over a branch the width of my arm. "The undergrowth makes it challenging. I'm surprised that they've made it as far as they have in the motor."

The engine cut off, and the noise of the wind whipping through the upper branches of the oaks and pines imitated the sound of a rushing river. We crept ahead to the bend in the road. Without speaking, we both moved to one side. Jasper held out a hand and helped me over a tree stump as we made our way to a stout oak with a wide trunk.

The Hispano-Suiza, its sides dirty and tires coated with mud and moss, sat near a rickety boathouse. Beyond it, the absence of trees and clear swath of star-speckled sky indicated the lake was straight ahead.

A torch beam sliced through the darkness. Our hands were still linked, and Jasper's grip tightened as the light played along the gaps in the boards of the boathouse. But the column of white didn't swing toward the woods. It fell to the ground, then bounced back and forth as someone walked away from the motor.

I squeezed Jasper's hand and nodded to a massive yew tree a little further along the road. He shook his head and jerked his thumb back down the lane in the direction of the ruined manor.

I frowned and went up on my tiptoes so I could whisper in his ear. "We've come all this way. Let's at least see what part of the lake they're going to, then we'll leave." I didn't give him a chance to reply. I crept forward until the massive gnarled trunk shielded me from being seen.

Jasper materialized beside me. "I want it on record that we should have left two minutes ago."

"Duly noted."

The wind didn't pick up again, and without it obscuring their words, Constance's voice, clear and distinct, carried back to us. " . . . if you'd buried it like I told you, we wouldn't even be here."

The man said something, but I couldn't quite hear him. His tone, however, was unmistakable. It was curt and cut across Constance's complaining tone.

"Why not?" she countered, her words audible. "It was all worked out. After you picked it up from the cloakroom, you should have gotten rid of it." Constance, still in her black evening cloak, came into sight. She stepped carefully as she came around the front of the motor, her arms held out from her sides for balance as she avoided patches of mud. "Why did you drive with it all the way back here? The idea was to get it as far from London as possible."

The man had been walking away from her, but now he half twisted back to face her. "I didn't know any isolated places in York, did I? You can't just stop by the side of the road and start digging. Besides, the ground is too hard at this time of year." He still pointed the torch toward the lake. Now that the light wasn't in front of him, I could see his face. "You didn't want to know anything about it at the time. I took care of it."

I leaned toward Jasper and kept my voice low. "That's Alec Woodwiss, the man Lola warned Diana about."

Constance had been moving along, but she slowed and sucked in a breath as she pressed her hand against the bonnet.

Alec swung the torch around and aimed it at Constance's face. "What's wrong?"

She threw up a hand to shield her eyes. "Stop that. You're blinding me."

The light dropped to the ground.

"Nothing's wrong," she said as she pushed away from the motor. She took a few steps, but she walked with one hand to her forehead. "Let's just get on with this. Show me where you put it."

The beam of light shifted back to the lake, glittering across the still water until it found the tip of a decaying dock that ran from the boathouse out several feet into the lake.

Alec said, "I chucked it off the end there, into the lake."

Constance halted, and her hand dropped. "You fool. Bodies float."

"I told you," Alec said. "I took care of it. I know better

243

than to just throw it in. I weighed it down with rocks, didn't I? There's no way anyone could have found it." Alec swung the torch across the surface of the lake. "See? Nothing."

Jasper touched my shoulder and tilted his head toward the darkness behind me. I nodded. We'd heard and seen enough. We could tell Longly exactly where to look for Lola's body. I shifted my footing, preparing to follow Jasper back down the lane.

Alec said, "No one's been here, either. You can tell by the ground." The light skipped along the mud and patchy grass. Jasper and I froze. The beam ranged across the tree trunks of the surrounding area, tracing over the yew we stood behind. My heart pounded, but the light didn't check, just swept on.

Jasper leaned in, his breath warm on my ear. "We'll wait until the wind picks up again, then we'll leave."

I nodded my agreement.

"We had to make sure." Constance took a few steps, her gait unsteady. "Give me the torch. I want to check."

I couldn't imagine picking one's way down the dock. It looked as if the boards might collapse at the slightest pressure. Alec muttered something but handed it over.

I looked up at the yew branches, willing the wind to slice through them and recreate that sound of a flowing river, which would cover any noise we made as we slipped away, but the treetop didn't stir.

Constance took a few steps toward the dock, then stumbled.

Alec caught her elbow. "Are you all right?" His voice wasn't as harsh.

"I'm fine. Just wobbly. Now, are you telling me that you walked on those decrepit-looking boards?"

"It's solid enough. I dragged the wretched trunk out there and tossed it off the end."

"After you weighed it down?" Constance sounded like a governess trying to detect if a child was lying.

"Yes."

"How?"

"I strapped some rather large rocks to it."

The torch beam played over the dock and across the water in an erratic manner. Constance put a hand to her head. "I don't feel so well."

Alec took the torch from her, wrapped an arm around her shoulders, and guided her to the boathouse. "Sit here for a moment until you feel better."

She dropped her head back against the worn boards of the building and closed her eyes. "I just need a moment. It's seeing the spot . . . knowing she's . . . out there somewhere underwater . . ."

"Of course." He walked away a few steps and took out a pack of cigarettes. The acrid smoke drifted in our direction, and I concentrated on taking shallow breaths. With my asthma, the last thing we needed was for me to have one of my coughing spells. What had happened to those wind gusts that had set branches clacking against each other a little earlier? We didn't dare move until the wind picked up again. If we took a step, they'd surely hear us. Jasper and I didn't need to consult with each other to know we had no choice. We stayed put.

After a few moments, Alec strolled back to the boathouse, his hands in his pockets. "Feeling better?"

"No, I don't know what's happening . . . I'm tired . . . and so . . . woozy."

He took a drag on his cigarette, then tossed it into the water. "That's the sleeping powder." He switched on the torch and tucked it under his arm, holding it in place so that it lit Constance up. She sat in an awkward angle, crumpled against the rough boards. She looked like an abandoned doll. Her head lolled to one side, and her arms draped loosely on either side, her gloves in the dirt.

Alec untied his bow tie. "Don't worry. It will help things go more smoothly."

"But . . . haven't taken . . . a powder." Stringing the words together into a sentence seemed to exhaust Constance.

"Yes, you have," Alec said briskly as he knelt beside her. "It was in the flask."

Constance shrugged, straining to sit straighter. But after a second, she gave up and collapsed back into her shrunken position. "But you . . . had some too . . ."

"I only pretended to drink from my flask." His tone was chiding.

"But . . . why?"

I had to strain to hear what she said.

"It's easier this way." Alec pulled her hands together and looped his tie around her wrists.

"What . . . Alec . . . ? What are you . . . doing?" Her slurred words were barely audible, and she didn't even make the effort to lift her head, which was tilted over to the side.

"Tying you up, my dear."

CHAPTER TWENTY-EIGHT

*J*asper and I exchanged a startled look at Alec's casual tone, but we didn't dare move. The wind hadn't picked up again. As soon as he finished tying Constance's hands together, Alec stood and took a gun from his jacket pocket.

I pressed my fingers to my mouth to stifle the gasp that welled up.

Alec looked down at Constance as he tapped the barrel of the gun against his trouser leg. "Why? Because I don't need you anymore."

She became slightly more animated and struggled into a position that wasn't quite so lopsided. "But we're . . . going away . . . together. With all of . . . Lola's lovely money. You need . . . me to . . . get it."

"No, I don't." He flung the gun in a casual gesture toward the Hispano-Suiza. "The key to your flat is in your handbag in the motor. I'll just tell the doorman you forgot it, that I'm running it up to you. It won't take me a moment to collect the bearer bonds you so helpfully removed from Lola's safety deposit box. Brilliant work fooling the bank manager, by the way. I'll take a little trip away from London in the Hispano-Suiza on my own." He lifted a shoulder. "It is a pity to leave before Lola's bank account has been completely drained, but the bonds and the motor aren't an insignificant haul."

A few moments before, Jasper and I had been poised to creep away, but we couldn't do that now, not with Alec waving a gun around in such a blasé manner. And no matter what Constance had done, we couldn't slip quietly away and leave her with Alec. Jasper motioned that he was going forward and I should stay put.

I sent him a message with my eyes that was a flat, *no!*

His shoulders heaved with a silent, exasperated sigh. Then he motioned for me to return up the lane toward the house, indicating he still wanted me to go off and leave him alone with a man with a gun.

I sent him an incredulous look. If he thought I'd leave him at a time like this, he was barmy. Not to mention that I didn't find the idea of tramping through the wilds of an abandoned country estate alone an attractive proposition.

Alec spoke to Constance again, waving the gun back and forth. "No, none of that. Tears won't move me. My mind is made up. I'm going away alone."

A whisper of air pushed against the back of my neck, ruffling my hair, and I tensed, waiting for the swoosh of a gust through the treetop, but the faint breeze died away to nothing.

Constance stopped struggling to right herself.

"Just . . . leave me." The pitiful request floated through the air, barely audible.

"Can't, my dear. Too risky. Yes, you're meek and terrified right now, but you'll be as angry as a wet cat when that sleeping powder wears off. You'll go straight to the police out of spite and tell them about me, even if it means a noose around your own neck." The cadence of his voice changed, and he spoke the next words more to himself than to Constance. "I'd thought shooting you would be the most expedient, but . . . no, I'll do it the same way I disposed of Lola."

Tree branches clicked overhead and a few leaves skittered, cartwheeling along the stretch of beach where the water lapped. The wind was picking up.

Alec put the gun away and picked up several rocks, which he dropped into the pockets of Constance's cloak. "Fitting, don't you think? You'll both rest at the bottom of the same lake. Granted, it will be a bit of an effort to get you to the end of the dock, but less messy overall than a gunshot. Have to think about these things. I don't want blood on me or in the motor."

A sharp gust of wind swished by, dislodging a branch. It clattered through the limbs and struck the ground a few inches in front of Jasper.

Alec spun toward the woods, stepping side to side as he raked the light over the trees. The spotlight of the torch beam landed on Jasper before he could dodge away from it. I was in the shadow of the tree and stayed there motionless, my heartbeat pounding in my ears as I dug my fingernails into the rough bark.

"You there! Come out!" Alec shouted.

Jasper didn't betray me by so much as a glance. He strolled forward, his steps weaving in an erratic route that took him away from the yew tree in a roughly diagonal line that moved him nearer Alec. "I say, that light is rather blinding. Be a good chap and lower it, why don't you?"

I leaned to the far side of the trunk and peeked out. Alec had turned slightly, following Jasper, which meant Alec and the gun were pointed slightly away from me. Since the light of the torch was aimed away from me now, I could see Alec had taken out the gun. The circle of light inched down to Jasper's chest, and I tried not to think about what an easy target the white of his shirt made.

"What are you doing here?"

Jasper ambled forward, his gait uneven, his words slurred as he said, "Looking for my blasted friends."

"Stop right there," Alec called, and Jasper tripped over a root. I tensed, afraid Alec would fire the gun, but Jasper righted himself, and his steps petered to a stop. The almost-fall had brought him within an arm's length of Alec. "Your friends?"

"Out for a bit of fun, don't you know. Wanted to see a ruined mansion in the moonlight." He looked around, his face vacant and benign. "I seem to have lost them. You haven't seen half a dozen Bright Young People wandering around, have you?"

"No. No one's been this way."

"Well then, if they haven't been here, I'll leave you. Got lost out here without a light of my own. If you point me in the direction of the road, I'll toddle along."

Alec flicked the light in the direction of the path. "Head that way. It'll take you back to the manor."

"Exce— Excell—" Jasper drew in a breath, swaying where he stood. "Very good," he amended. "If only I'd thought to bring a torch. It would help quite a bit." Jasper gave the word *torch* a particular emphasis, and it was as if he'd spoken to me. I knew what he intended.

I yanked the torch out of my pocket. Jasper half turned as if he was going to stumble away. I clicked on the torch and aimed it at Alec's face, temporarily blinding him. Jasper closed the distance and delivered a right hook that sent Alec spinning away. He landed and lay motionless on the ground, his cheek pressed to the dirt.

I rushed forward. Jasper was shaking out his hand. "Well done, picking up on my hints, Olive. Well done, indeed."

"What were you thinking, walking right up to a man with a gun? You can't take that kind of risk! It was absurd and foolhardy and impetuous and . . . and—don't you ever do anything like that again."

Jasper stopped massaging his hand and smiled at me. "I think that's the nicest thing you've ever said to me, Olive. Thank you." He kissed me, and I gripped his shoulders. All the adrenaline and worry and pent-up energy coursing through me channeled itself into our kiss.

It was quite a kiss. Eventually we broke apart. Jasper said, "Oh my." He stepped back and looked around as if he'd forgotten where he was. I know I certainly had. "Right." He cleared his throat. "Well. Although I'd rather kiss you again, we'd better see to these two."

"Don't think this discussion is over," I said, but the angry heat had gone out of my voice. "I have rather a lot to say to you."

"And I'll be delighted to listen. We've only had a few really good rows. If that kiss was any indication, we should have a few more—as long as we can make up like that." Jasper loosened his bow tie, leaned down, and used it to secure Alec's hands behind his back. "Poetic justice, don't you think?"

"Very appropriate," I said and made my way over to Constance.

Jasper said, "I'll collect the gun and hold it for the police. In case he comes around, we don't want any complications."

I checked on Constance. Her head rested on her shoulder, and her eyes were closed. Mascara smudges ringed her eyes and streaked the powder on her face where her tears had run down to her chin. She looked pitiful and helpless, but I couldn't feel very sorry for her. She was a murderess, after all. I pressed my fingers against her neck, then stepped back and went to where Jasper stood over Alec. "Constance is out, but she is still breathing. We need a doctor."

"And the police," Jasper added.

"Good idea," a voice behind us announced.

We both turned. "Inspector Longly!" I said, my heart surging back into a frantic pace. "What are you doing here?"

"Following a lead."

"So you didn't close the case."

"Far from it. I wasn't satisfied. We've been shadowing Miss Duskin all day while checking on Woodwiss. Pair of 'bad 'uns,' as they say. But this does wrap up everything nicely." He turned, and, at his signal, several uniformed police officers stepped out of the woods. "Jolly good show facing off with Woodwiss, Rimington, but there was no need for it. You were in our line of sight the whole time, or we would have shown ourselves sooner."

"You overheard Alec and Constance?" I asked.

"Yes. I didn't want to—er—interrupt your moment—um —earlier. We held back, but we were hidden in the woods." He grinned in a way that I'd never seen. He looked almost . . . cheeky. Yes, that was it. I felt a blush rising. Longly cleared his throat and shifted back to his businesslike tone. "I had a man trace Woodwiss' movements over the last week. When I learned Woodwiss had traveled to York earlier this week, I put a man on him today. In fact, he was seated beside Woodwiss and Miss Duskin in Rules, so he knew their destination tonight."

A police officer came and stood over Alec, and another went to hover over Constance. Longly broke off and called out to an officer to check the Hispano-Suiza. "Secure Miss Duskin's handbag, Mills, then round up a doctor."

Longly turned back to us. "We had a devil of a time avoiding you and keeping our presence from Woodwiss and Duskin tonight. But we can chat about all this in the next day or so. I have to stay here and oversee the removal of these two and"—he gestured to the water as a grim look traced across his features—"have a look in the lake. It will likely take quite some time. Perhaps you would like to return to London? You've had quite a night."

CHAPTER TWENTY-NINE

*M*iss Bobbin wrote down the final score for the rubber and put down her pencil. "Nicely done, Olive. Thank you for partnering with me."

"It was my pleasure." I was relieved I'd acquitted myself fairly well during the game. When one is matched up with a bridge instructor, it's enough to rattle one's nerves.

Miss Bobbin pushed back her chair. "Shall we take a break? Refreshments are in the dining room."

It felt rather strange to think that last night, Jasper and I had crept around the grounds of Astwick Manor, and now we were attending a bridge party where the only sounds were the crackle of the fire from the sitting room, the shuffling of cards, and the gentle murmur among the players.

I'd been surprised to see that all current residents of the second floor—except Mr. Underhill, of course—were in attendance along with several of Miss Bobbin's bridge students.

Minerva had been partnered with Mr. Culpepper, and

their group was also moving away from the table. Minerva said a brief word to him, then signaled to me that she would meet me by the fireplace. I nodded, picked up my teacup, took a macaron, and made my way through the scattered tables.

When I returned from Astwick, I'd told Minerva everything that had happened, but there were still gaps in our knowledge of what had happened with Lola. When we'd arrived that evening, there hadn't been time for chitchat. Miss Bobbin had been intent on organizing everyone into their places and starting the bridge games.

"Inspector Longly stopped by this afternoon, and now I know more," Minerva said as soon as she was by my side.

"Kudos to you. He's never very forthcoming with me. What did you find out?"

"The most important—and disturbing—thing is that they found Lola's body in the lake."

"So Alec wasn't lying about what he did."

"Did you think he was?"

"I had no idea. He told Constance that Lola's body was in the lake, but he's not exactly the reliable sort."

"He's a thoroughly despicable person. And he comes from quite a good family too. Younger son. Apparently up until a few years ago, he was only a bit aimless, but then he fell into a pattern of mooching off women."

"Diana told me he tried to do that with Lola, but she wasn't having any of it."

"Inspector Longly confirmed that. He said Constance has held nothing back. She told Longly that when Alec realized he wouldn't be able to get any money out of Lola, he dropped her. Then Alec and Constance created a plan to get Lola's money. It was exactly as you thought. Once they'd gotten Lola out of the way, Constance would play the part of Lola to get access to her bank accounts."

I'd picked up the macaron, but now I put it down on the saucer of my teacup. I'd lost my appetite. "But he wasn't very loyal, was he? Alec was also courting Diana during that time."

"He was every bit the cad that Lola said he was."

We were silent a moment. All I could think of was Lola, caught up in the scheme of two grasping people. "Did Longly say anything about the case against Constance and Alec?"

"He did. With Constance sharing all the details of what she and Alec did, Inspector Longly says they'll stand trial. Constance realized that with the Kemps moving out, it was the perfect opportunity to create an alibi. Constance drowned Lola in the bath, then wrapped the body in the rug from the living room. She put the rug in the hall while the maid cleaned, then after the maid finished, she brought the rug back inside the flat. Once Evans brought up the trunk, she put the body in it. She took it as her luggage on the Flying Scotsman, but she got off in York, just as you and Jasper thought. She left the trunk in the cloak room at the station, but Alec was waiting for her there. She gave him the ticket for the trunk before she returned to London. He picked up the trunk."

"And didn't follow Constance's plan of burying it. I wonder why he took it to Astwick? It is a deserted place and he could be fairly sure of privacy there, but how did he hit on that place?"

"Longly says Alec grew up in the area. He must have been aware of the lake."

"Imagine having Evans move the trunk out of the building, then taking it on the Flying Scotsman, bold as you please," I said, my mind boggling with the intricate timing and the sheer daring of their plan. "They'd worked out all the details, hadn't they?"

"Even down to making sure to put the rug back," Minerva said. "Constance draped it over two chairs and put it in front of the fire to dry it. It would have been soaked with bath water. Then she returned the rug to its usual place on the floor in the sitting room as if nothing had happened! It's just ghastly and cold-blooded."

"It is." I couldn't quite suppress the wave of revulsion that rolled through me at the thought of what had happened in the flat next door to me.

"I'd thought I might want a roommate someday, but this has put me off the idea altogether," Minerva said. "Except for you, Olive," she added quickly. "I'd trust you implicitly."

"And I feel the same. Although, I'm not ready to move house and live with someone else. I'm quite enjoying my solitary splendor."

Diana, who was still seated at a table where a game was wrapping up, let out a small squeal of delight. Monty was her partner, and he nodded with satisfaction. Jasper, who was also at the same table and had been partnered with one of Miss Bobbin's students, groaned. He clapped Monty on the shoulder, then nodded to Diana and the other lady as he pushed back from the table.

I had news, of my own. "Did you know that Diana intends to sponsor fundraising drives for the two charities Lola had me research?"

Minerva's eyes narrowed. "Diana? Involved in charity work?"

"Yes. She heard the news about Lola's death and came straight over to see me today. She was quite shaken and distraught. She wanted to apologize to Lola after their argument, but she'll never have the chance."

"But how did she know about the charities?" Minerva asked. "That detail isn't common knowledge."

"I told her." My client confidentiality concerns were at an end. All my interactions with Lola would be in the police report, and they'd become public during the trials of Alec and Constance. "I hinted that a donation in Lola's name would be appreciated. It was the only thing I could think to suggest. A few hours later, I was taking calls from the matrons on the boards of the charities. They were thrilled with Diana's plans. She'd not only made two rather large donations, she's also taken the charities as her own projects."

"Well, Diana certainly doesn't waste any time, does she?" Minerva said as Jasper came across the room and joined us.

He asked, "Have either of you seen the evening paper? No? Then you'll be interested in the article on the front page."

He took a newspaper from his inside jacket pocket. It

was folded into fourths. He opened it and revealed a head-line in a large font, *MP Keeps Love Nest in Bloomsbury.*

Minerva leaned forward. "That's a picture of South Regent Mansions."

Jasper handed her the paper. "Indeed it is. Underhill's former ladylove has granted an interview. It has all the things that the reading public enjoys—a secret passage, subterfuge, and scandal. Makes for fascinating reading."

Peering over Minerva's shoulder, I asked, "What happened? Why is she talking to the newspapers now?"

"Apparently Underhill broke it off. She wasn't pleased and"—Jasper tapped a small line at the end of the article—"her new show opens tomorrow."

Minerva said, "Well, Evans will have his hands full now. The reporters will be setting up camp in the park, staking out the building."

"You'd better not let them know you live here, Minerva," I said. "All the reporters at *The Hullabaloo* will want to use you to get inside."

"Heaven forbid. I might have to ask Evans to put the basement door to good use and let me enter and leave that way until the interest dies down."

"It will certainly make things in the political realm inter-esting," Jasper said as Minerva reached to hand the paper back to him.

I intercepted her. "May I? I haven't seen the Beatrice cartoon today."

"Actually, you have seen this one. It's the final version of the one about Beatrice's driving passions."

"I liked that one," I said as I turned the pages to find it.

"The wife of the editor of *The Express* also liked it." Minerva's tone indicated there was more to the story.

"Did she?" I asked.

"Very much so. In fact, she's been a fan of mine for some time. She told her husband—quite often, apparently—that he was a fool if he didn't lure me away from *The Hullabaloo.* He took her advice and telephoned me this afternoon. He offered me a job at *The Express.*"

"That's wonderful—as long as it's a good offer," I said.

"It's an extremely good offer. I told him I wasn't willing to move unless I had complete control of the content of the Beatrice comic and that I must be able to work independently and report directly to him. He agreed."

I raised my teacup. "How wonderful. Congratulations!"

"Thank you." She raised her teacup. "Here's to saying goodbye to old Harrison on Monday."

"Cheers to that." I handed the paper back to her. "You'll want to keep this, then," I said with a glance at Jasper, who nodded his approval of me giving away his newspaper.

"Whatever for?" Minerva asked.

"For your archive."

Something over my shoulder had distracted her, but her attention snapped back to me. "My archive? Are you mad? Archives are for serious people like poets and playwrights. I'll never have an archive."

"I wouldn't be too sure of that," I said. "Women cartoonists are a rather rare breed. I'm convinced that someday your sketches and notes will be in some university. Scholars will study them."

"Don't be silly."

SARA ROSETT

"I'm entirely serious and mean every word I've said. In fact, I should collect a few autographs from you."

Minerva laughed. "Well, it's a nice idea, even if it's rather far-fetched." Her gaze again focused on a point over my shoulder near the dining room table. I shifted to see what interested her. Mr. Culpepper was the only person in the dining room. When I swiveled in his direction, he turned away, pushed up his glasses with his index finger, and gave the macarons an intense study.

Minerva jiggled my arm. "Don't scare him away, Olive. I've worked hard to get him to this point."

I spun back to her. "What point?"

"He's asked me to dinner."

"How intriguing. Did you say yes?"

"I did. I'm thinking of a new storyline for the comic. I think Beatrice might encounter a scientist or inventor type. I can see several possible storylines that could emerge from that situation. I had to say yes . . . for research purposes alone."

"I think Mr. Culpepper could be a big fan of research."

"I certainly hope so." She hefted her saucer. "Oh, look, I'm out of tea. I think I need another cup."

She joined Mr. Culpepper, and they fell into conversation. Neither of them refilled their teacups.

"Speaking of interesting alliances . . ." I said to Jasper as I tilted my head in the direction of Miss Bobbin and Mr. Popinjay, who were chatting amicably. "What has happened there? Who would have ever thought that they would get along so nicely?" Ace trotted up and sniffed Mr. Popinjay's

262

ankle, and he leaned down to rub the dog's ears. "Have they declared a truce?"

Jasper said, "I believe it has to do with Mrs. Attenborough's early departure this evening."

"I noticed she left. What was that about?"

"Miss Bobbin and Mr. Popinjay were partnered together in a bridge game earlier this evening. Someone sent their regrets at the last minute, and there was no choice but for them to pair up and fill the last table. They took on Mrs. A and her partner. It turns out they are a force to be reckoned with when it comes to bridge."

"You're still speaking of Miss Bobbin and Mr. Popinjay?"

"Yes. Mrs. A made a few disparaging remarks at the beginning of play about bridge instructors. Apparently, Mrs. A rarely loses, or so she says, and *she's* never had to take lessons. She also mentioned how much she dislikes cats and called them *mangy*. It turns out Mr. Popinjay is quite good at bridge."

"So Miss Bobbin and Mr. Popinjay worked together? As partners?" I repeated, still trying to take it in.

"Yes," Jasper said.

"What was the result?"

"Utter annihilation. It was quite a sight. Mrs. A was thoroughly trounced. She suddenly remembered she had an urgent telephone call that she had to make."

"Well, that's a turn I didn't expect."

Miss Bobbin went to answer a knock at her door, and I said, "Perhaps that's Mrs. Attenborough back for a rematch."

But Miss Bobbin returned alone. She carried a letter and threaded her way through the knots of people to Jasper.

"Just arrived for you, Mr. Rimington. Evans sent the delivery boy straight up with it."

"Thank you." Jasper looked at the address and said to himself, "Yes, Grigsby would know I'd want to see this at once and send it on to me here." He ripped open the envelope and scanned the lines.

I watched his face, but it didn't give anything away. "Not bad news, I hope."

"No, rather the opposite." He looked up. "I've been invited on a trip. It's a group tour. What do you say to a holiday?"

"I find that a very interesting proposition. I'd like to hear more."

THE END

Sign up for Sara's updates at SaraRosett.com/signup to get exclusive content and early excerpts from her books.

THE STORY BEHIND THE STORY

*T*hank you for joining Olive on another adventure. I always enjoy traveling back to the 1920s. It's a nice escape from the problems and stress of the modern world.

Inspiration for this novel came partly from the research I did into life in 1920s London and also from Agatha Christie's short story, *The Third Floor Flat*, along with the Poirot television episode of the same name. Christie fans will have noticed my hat-tip to Christie's book, *Why Didn't They Ask Evans?* I intentionally picked the name of Evans for the head porter in the story as an acknowledgement of Christie's puzzle mysteries, which have inspired me.

I went down several research "rabbit holes" while writing *Murder at the Mansions*, including a deep dive on female cartoonists of the early twentieth century. *The Flapper Queens: Women Cartoonists of the Jazz Age* by Trina Robbins gave me a look at the beautiful art of female cartoonists. Originally, I'd planned to include more details about Minerva's work as a cartoonist, but the story became more focused on South Regent Mansions so those details would have weighed down the narrative. If you have an interest, check out some of the early woman cartoonists like Nell Brinkley and Fay King as well as Ethel Hays, whose Flapper Fanny cartoon inspired the Beatrice cartoons.

I also found some fascinating information on the Flying Scotsman—although it was much easier to discover details about the engine named the Flying Scotsman, which has some rather ardent fans, rather than the train journey. You can still travel the route of the Flying Scotsman, but it only takes a little over four hours and the trains aren't so elegant as they were in Olive's day. The food service and interior of the train coaches have changed as well. Sadly, I didn't get to make the rail journey in person. I wrote *Murder at the Mansions* while COVID-19 was limiting travel, but I did make the journey vicariously through books and YouTube.

When I plotted this novel, I worked out how the murder was committed and how the body was moved, which included brainstorming how the villains would use the train station's left luggage, or cloakroom as it was known in the 1920s. It was only when I was about halfway into the writing of the book that I learned about the famous "trunk murders" of the 1930s, which involved luggage left at Brighton station and King's Cross station. Deeper research revealed that a case dubbed The Bungalow Murder, which occurred in 1924, also involved leaving evidence at a train station, this time Waterloo.

On a lighter note, you can still dine at Rules in London and join the long list of famous patrons that includes

Charles Dickens, Charlie Chaplin, Clark Gable, and members of the royal family.

And if you're interested in manor house ruins, an internet search will bring up plenty of homes that were abandoned. With the increase in death duties and the economic changes of the 1920s, many country mansions were destroyed or abandoned because the families couldn't afford the upkeep. Some, like my fictional Astwick Manor, are slowly being reclaimed by nature. I found the site Lost-Heritage.org.uk especially helpful when it came to creating my fictional Astwick manor house ruin.

Olive will be back in another adventure soon. If you'd like a note when the next book is coming out, please sign up for my updates at SaraRosett.com/signup. You'll also get my personal mystery book recommendations as well as exclusive content and giveaways.

ABOUT THE AUTHOR

USA Today bestselling author Sara Rosett writes light-hearted mysteries for readers who enjoy atmospheric settings, fun characters, and puzzling whodunits. She loves reading Golden Age mysteries, watching Jane Austen adaptions, and travel.

She is the author of the High Society Lady Detective historical mystery series as well as three contemporary cozy series: the Murder on Location series, the On the Run series, and the Ellie Avery series. Sara is the creator of an online course, How to Outline A Cozy Mystery, and the author of *How to Write a Series*. Her nonfiction for readers includes *The Bookish Sleuth: Mystery Reader's Journal and Planner.*

Publishers Weekly called Sara's books "enchanting," "well-executed," and "sparkling." Sara loves to get new stamps in her passport and considers dark chocolate a daily requirement. Find out more at SaraRosett.com.

Connect with Sara
www.SaraRosett.com